CW00469636

TIME HUNTER
DEUS LE VOLT

TIME HUNTER
DEUS LE VOLT

Jon De Burgh Miller

TIME HUNTER #8

First published in England in 2005 by
Telos Publishing Ltd,
139 Whitstable Road, Canterbury, Kent CT2 8EQ
www.telos.co.uk

This Edition 2020

Telos Publishing Ltd values feedback. Please e-mail us with
any comments you may have about this book to:
feedback@telos.co.uk

ISBN: 978-1-84583-150-9

Deus Le Volt © 2005, 2020 Jon De Burgh Miller

Time Hunter format © 2003 Telos Publishing Ltd.
Honoré Lechasseur and Emily Blandish
created by Daniel O'Mahony.
The Fendahl created by Chris Boucher and used with
permission.

The moral rights of the author have been asserted.

British Library Cataloguing in Publication Data.
A catalogue record for this book is available from the British
Library.

This book is sold subject to the condition that it shall not by
way of trade or otherwise, be lent, resold, hired out or
otherwise circulated without the publisher's prior written
consent in any form of binding or cover other than that in
which it is published and without a similar condition
including this condition being imposed on the subsequent
purchaser.

The Time Hunter

Honoré Lechasseur and Emily Blandish ... Honoré is a black American ex-GI, now living in London, 1950, working sometimes as a private detective, sometimes as a 'fixer', or spiv. Now life has a new purpose for him as he has discovered that he is a time sensitive. In theory, this attribute, as well as affording him a low-level perception of the fabric of time itself, gives him the ability to sense the whole timeline of any person with whom he comes into contact. He just has to learn how to master it.

Emily is a strange young woman whom Honoré has taken under his wing. She is suffering from amnesia, and so knows little of her own background. She comes from a time in Earth's far future, one of a small minority of people known as time channellers, who have developed the ability to make jumps through time using mental powers so highly evolved that they could almost be mistaken for magic. They cannot do this alone, however. In order to achieve a time-jump, a time channeller must connect with a time sensitive.

When Honoré and Emily connect, the adventures begin.

Dedication

To my Grandad, Robert Clubley, who encouraged me from a young age to take an interest in all things historical.

1

It was a hot summer's night in London, the sort of night when it's physically impossible to sleep. The sort of night when it can feel as if something primal inside you is doing everything it can to stop you falling into a dream, to stop you facing the twilight world between the conscious and unconscious.

Honoré Lechasseur knew he wouldn't be sleeping much that night, but the heat would have little to do with it. Being a spiv was a trade he had perfected years ago, after his wartime injuries had healed, but change was in the air.

The end of rationing was the cause of celebration for most of London, but the life of a spiv became far less lucrative. Gone were the days when bars of chocolate and boxes of bananas could be traded for a very healthy profit. It was getting to the stage where the only real money was in drugs or weapons, something Honoré really didn't want to get wrapped up in. He knew it wouldn't be long before he faced the choice between stepping over the line between legal and illegal once and for all, or finding a new trade to pay his rent and fill his days. Still, that was in the future. For now, there was just enough work around to keep him out of trouble; but it was getting harder and harder, so he had to be careful. The worry was playing on his mind more than usual that night.

He finished up the deal with his supplier and handed the cash over in exchange for a few anonymous boxes wrapped in brown paper. Twelve cartons of cigarettes, the extra strong kind from Eastern Europe, smuggled through in the hold of a ferry and whisked away before customs guards could get a look in. Honoré loaded the boxes into his backpack and shook hands with his client. He gave a tip of the hat and a nod of the head, the standard way to acknowledge a successful transaction. The two men walked away in deliberately opposite directions. It always paid to be cautious, although there was rarely anyone around at this time of night. It would soon be morning, however. A few eager birds were already warming their lungs up for the dawn chorus.

Honoré looked at his watch. Emily should be there by now. She'd been running an errand in Aldwych, after which she was supposed to meet him on the corner of Marchmont and Bernard Street. He was in the right place, but there was no sign of his friend.

Honoré sighed to himself. What kind of life was this? Even Emily was getting dragged into it now, and that wasn't fair on her. Perhaps it was time to find a new career? They had talked about setting up some kind of legitimate business together, but neither had much of an idea what trade or service they could offer that would make enough money to justify the effort. Honoré had toyed with the idea of using his special gift, the ability to see glimpses of a person's past and future just by concentrating, to become a fortune teller, but the idea of wearing a headscarf, makeup and large earrings while spending his days staring at crystal balls held little appeal.

Honoré's train of thought was broken by a loud retort that echoed around the empty streets. At first he thought it might be an explosion, and pressed himself against a wall. Above him, a ball of light and electrical energy was suspended several storeys high above the ground, filling the street with jumping shadows. Before he could figure out what the phenomenon was, he heard an agonised cry and saw a figure fall from the ball of energy and land on the ground with a crunching thud. There was a moment's silence, and the energy ball vanished as suddenly as it had appeared. Honoré looked at the body in the street, and started when it moaned gently and tried to move. He threw down his backpack and ran over to see if he could help. The figure was an elderly man with pale skin, a long, white beard and thin, wispy hair. His chest was covered by a polished metal sheet, and Honoré suddenly realised that he was wearing a medieval suit of armour. He was still breathing and murmuring, but seemed on the verge of slipping into unconsciousness.

'Hold on,' Honoré said. 'I'll get help.'

'Get me out,' the man moaned. 'Get me out of here!'

'Take it easy, you'll be safe soon. We'll get you to a hospital.'

Honoré expected that his words would reassure the man, but they seemed to have the opposite effect. The man opened his eyes and stared at Honoré with a shocked look. 'You should not be here! Leave me alone, infidel!'

Honoré shook his head. The man was delirious, but the fiery intensity of his eyes and the clear look of recognition on his face were chilling.

'I will kill you this time!' the man growled as Honoré stood up.

Fighting the extreme pain he must have been suffering, the man managed to sit up, then reached out and grabbed Honoré's leg, before slowly falling back to the ground.

A wave of imagery assailed Honoré, his mind touching the injured man's soul and tearing out memory after memory from his life.

Honoré saw a vast desert, a shining row of castle battlements standing firm through a sandstorm. He saw vast armies of soldiers on horseback, some in medieval suits of armour and others in filthy smocks. He saw terrified women running through blood-filled streets carrying their babies, and he saw a chapel, a bright light, and a Pope preaching for all of Europe to go on a glorious crusade. An expedition to rid the Holy Land of the heathen forces of the Turks and Saracens who were using the holy places of Christendom for debauchery and devil-worship. Honoré saw the crowd respond excitedly to the Pope's words, fired up and inspired by what they'd heard. And in that crowd, Honoré saw a young man fall to his knees, weeping as he came to understand his destiny. And then his vision changed, and he saw nothing but darkness. He felt a sense of loneliness, of torment, and of death. Honoré snapped away fast, fearful of what he would see next.

He turned away from the man, breathing heavily, his heart thumping. The suit of armour was genuine. The man was some kind of knight from the past.

Emily came running round the corner of the street, clearly in a hurry. Honoré was thrilled to see her. He knew that her interest would be more than a little piqued by the discovery.

'Sorry I'm late,' she said. Then she saw the body. 'Oh my God. What happened?'

Honoré pointed heavenwards. 'This guy just fell out of the sky.'

Emily looked up at him, not understanding. 'What? We need to get him some help!'

'I saw his past. He's some sort of knight from hundreds of years ago.'

Emily laughed; then, as she realised he was being serious, her look turned to one of incredulity. She turned her attention back to the man and reached down to feel his armour. 'Either that or the circus is in town.'

The man gasped for air, then closed his eyes.

'I think he's like you, Emily. Somehow he's managed to travel through time. And the strange thing is, he seemed to recognise me, and seemed determined to kill me.'

Emily stood up and took a couple of paces back, her eyes wide as the implications of her friend's words sank in.

'We have to get him to a hospital,' continued Honoré. 'Otherwise, he could well die.'

Emily's voice dropped to a whisper. 'I don't think it's wise to hand him over to the authorities. If he is a time traveller, we should find out who he is and how he came to be here. If we go back to wherever he came from, then we may get a better idea what it is we're dealing with.'

Honoré nodded as he thought this through. 'Come on then,' he said eventually. 'Let's do it.'

He knelt down and touched one hand to the knight's shoulder, feeling his soul reach nine hundred and fifty years into the past. He reached his other hand up and clasped it tightly into Emily's palm. Emily closed her eyes, and a spark of energy fizzed between the two. Honoré could feel Emily channelling the temporal winds through her body, pulling herself across time and taking him with her. He felt the knight's time snake rippling back, and while most of what he saw was a blur, he was instinctively aware of the point he needed to visualise, an image he hoped was no more than a few weeks before the knight had travelled through time.

And then the maelstrom of colour faded, to be replaced with a bright wash of light as reality coalesced to reveal a stark, rugged landscape. Laid out before them was a vast fortressed city, and around it a large encampment of tents and huts of all shapes and sizes. Honoré looked at Emily as the heat from the sun beat down on them.

Where exactly had they arrived this time …?

2

Deep within the heart of the city lay a Christian church. Rarely used, and desecrated many years earlier, it now played host to a man who stood in luxurious robes, addressing a ragtag group of mongrel pilgrims.

'For too long we have been made to wait,' he declared. 'For too long we have been made to suffer while our leaders argue amongst themselves, unable to make a single decision.'

He looked skyward, his eyes wide with fervour. 'Those times are over. The time for us to act is now. My family is blessed with a special gift, a Holy Spirit of power that man was not meant to possess, a power passed down from the time of King David, through followers of Christ throughout the ages who knew that their way was the true way forward, the true Holy Spirit. I have been chosen as the one who will herald the return of a beast of unimaginable power, from the Book of Revelation itself.'

'Master,' one of the pilgrims said, concern evident on his face. 'I have heard stories of this creature. Few survive its presence.'

The robed man nodded. 'None of us will survive this. Not in this life. But in the next, we will do more than live. We will live for eternity in paradise. We will rule over the firmament, seated at the right hand of the new ruler of Heaven. My ancestors were told by Christ himself that they were his brothers, and now we know what he meant by that.'

The man held out a scrap of velvet cloth, on which sat a large fragment of bone. His eyes burned passionately, and his mouth twitched into a yellowing grin. 'Soon the whole world will tremble before the might of my master!'

As the scorching rays of sunlight beat down on her back, Emily Blandish cursed the fact that she'd been wearing such a thick dress when they'd made the jump back in time. She looked at Honoré with envy. He hadn't had any more time to plan for this trip than she had, yet in his regular clothes – white shirt and light grey trousers under a leather coat and hat – he was dressed much more appropriately for the conditions. He had quickly taken his hat and coat off, despite the hat's useful sun shading properties, and was carrying them under his arm. If this was as far back in time as they suspected, the last thing they wanted was to look too anachronistic.

They'd found themselves standing on a rough desert hillock. Crimson sand dominated the landscape, punctuated by clumps of brownish green plant life. The area was strewn with rocks, many of which looked like the ruins of what had once been defence structures.

'You could have put us down in a better spot than this,' chided Emily.

'I didn't manage to stop the jump where I wanted,' Honoré admitted, 'so we may end up having to search for a bit before we find our man.'

Emily could think of better news to receive at that point. 'Well then,' she said, putting on a brave face, 'the sooner we make friends with the locals, the better.'

In the distance ahead of them was an imposing mountain range, lined with structures that were presumably defensive forts of some kind, while at the base of the range was the vast city, which even from this distance, approximately half a mile away, Emily could tell contained a rich variety of architectural styles and influences.

The collection of dwellings around the city reminded Emily of a refugee camp she'd seen when she and Honoré had gone travelling in Africa recently. It was made up of rows of dilapidated tents of every conceivable shape and size, with thoroughfares in between them that bustled with people. Emily estimated that it would take at least twenty minutes to walk from one end of the camp to the other.

'I could do with getting out of this heat,' Lechasseur said, as they set off toward the dwellings.

Emily agreed. 'I'll roast like a Sunday dinner if I don't find something more suitable to change into soon. And we'll stick out like a sore thumb if we stay in these clothes.'

They soon reached the outskirts of the camp, and Lechasseur shot Emily a look that told her to be on her guard. As they moved forward, Emily could see that the place was a hive of activity. Women and children were busy digging through the barren ground in search of scraps of food, while rows of washed smocks were being hung out to dry in the stark desert air. Groups of men dressed in dirty red tunics and wearing knee-length boots were clustered around the entrances to their tents, presumably discussing their plans for the day, whilst a great many malnourished horses, donkeys, dogs and camels wandered aimlessly around the camp, looking for a purpose, trying to understand why their masters had subjected them to such hardship.

Adding to the unpleasantness was the foulest stench Emily had ever had the misfortune to be exposed to, which became stronger the further they moved into the camp. Many-weeks-stale human sweat mixed with a concoction of several different types of animal faeces and rotten vegetables created an atmosphere that must have been an absolute dream for the clouds of flies and mosquitoes that hovered all around. 'Why are we doing this?' Lechasseur asked, gagging at the stench. 'We could just go back and try some other time.'

Emily smiled and shook her head. 'Come on, be strong,' she urged. 'We'll get used to it, I'm sure! When in Rome ...'

'... things smell a whole lot nicer than they do here!' Lechasseur finished. 'You don't fool anyone, Emily. And one thing's for sure. I'll never complain about the smell of London again.'

The locals were starting to give them some suspicious looks, so the two travellers ducked out of sight round the side of a large tent. There they found a small dry ditch, into which Lechasseur bundled his coat and hat, along with his watch.

Emily took off her blouse, which she had been wearing beneath her dress, but realised she would have to keep the dress itself until she found more suitable clothes. Lechasseur kicked some earth down onto the bundle, concealing it from sight.

Once they had hidden their clothes, they moved round to the front of the tent again, where a boy of about twelve stood next to a horse. Although he was covered in grime, his skin betrayed the lobster red of someone pale who had not adjusted well to an existence in the sun. The boy was grooming the horse with a metal comb, vainly attempting to remove a tick that had decided to take up residence in the animal's fur.

'Hello,' Emily said gently as she walked up to the boy, closely followed by Lechasseur. 'I wonder if you could help us.'

The boy looked up, and his previous expression of disinterest was replaced by one of alarm, his eyes widening at the sight of the two travellers.

'Who are you?' he whispered fearfully. 'You're not going to kill me, are you?' Emily presumed his reaction was due to their clothes still being somewhat out of place.

Lechasseur raised a hand in a friendly manner. 'Relax. We won't harm you. We're just looking for a friend of ours. We just want to speak to someone in charge.'

The boy made the sign of the cross on his chest and looked up towards the sky. 'Father, forgive me my sins and remove the blight of your enemies from my life.' He looked back towards the visitors, took a few deep breaths, then stood up straight as if mimicking a gesture he had seen the grown-ups adopt in formal situations. 'You are from the city?' he asked.

Lechasseur and Emily looked at each other. They needed an alibi. Emily just hoped it was one that would be well received. 'Yes, we're from the city,' she replied.

The boy frowned then shook his head. 'May God have mercy on your souls, and your heathen idols stay forever fallen.' He tied a rope loosely around his horse's neck and secured it to a tent pole. 'I see you are bearing no weapons,' he said, 'though I have heard your like have magic rituals that can deceive pure Christian souls into believing what is not real. Follow me, and if you let me live, I will take you to my master.'

3

As they walked through the camp, Emily's desire to change clothes intensified, not just because of the heat of the day, but because it became increasingly clear how out of place she looked. She didn't know whether it was a white girl accompanying a black man or her unusual dress sense that made people stare more, but either way, it was clear that nobody in the camp had seen anything quite like them before. The natives seemed to be dressed very simply, in drably coloured rags and what looked like sheepskin tunics or crop sacks that must have itched like hell. From time to time she saw someone wearing cleaner, brighter-coloured clothes than most and realised this must be one of the superior figures among the group, but for the most part they looked a motley and pathetic bunch.

'Who are you taking us to?' Emily asked the boy.

'You're in the camp of Godfrey de Bouillion,' the boy replied, his voice shaking. 'He is the Duke of Lower Lorraine and holder of more armies and fiefdoms than the rest of the holy princes put together.'

They walked past several large tents, the standard of dress improving with every group of people they saw, until finally the boy stopped outside a tent with a crude yet intimidating red cross painted on the side in what Emily suspected was blood. She guessed the symbol did not mean that this was the first-aid tent.

The boy paused before drawing back a cloth blanket that was covering the entrance. 'If you so much as breathe in the wrong direction when in the presence of my master,' he warned, doing his best to sound intimidating, 'then you will both be killed.'

The boy moved through the entrance, and Lechasseur and

Emily followed.

Inside the tent, Emily could see that the structure had been partitioned into different areas, each serving a different purpose depending on the time of day. Most of the tent appeared to be designed for sleeping, with rags strewn out across the ground and several men lying down upon them, like the destitutes one occasionally saw picking through Blitz rubble in the East End.

In one corner of the room, a group of children played while their mother watched on, making a futile attempt to suckle a heartbreakingly pathetic-looking baby that, based on its size and skeletal definition, Emily was sure wouldn't stand a chance of surviving more than a few days.

The boy led them further into the tent, to a large, open area with a small table in the middle. A burly, shirtless man in his early forties, with an unruly grey beard that spread down to his chest and a sheepskin garment around his waist, was standing at the head of the table, giving orders to a group of emaciated younger men who were struggling to get into heavy-looking tarnished chain mail vests.

'Forgive me, master' the boy said. 'I have something to show you.'

The men looked up. Gasps and mutterings rippled across the room as they saw the unusual visitors.

The large man marched over to Lechasseur. 'A heathen minion, in my camp?' He looked down at the boy and grabbed him by the scruff of his shirt. 'What in the Lord's name do you think you are doing, bringing such a wretched and specimen into my home?'

'I ... I'm sorry sir,' the boy said fearfully. 'He came from the city. I thought perhaps you could use him, to set a trap for the devils?'

The man seemed to think about this for a few seconds, then let go of the boy, who fell to the ground and scrabbled away, out of arm's reach.

'I'm sorry, master,' the boy said, but Godfrey wasn't listening. He had turned his attention toward Emily, circling her as if eyeing a cut of meat. He placed a hand softly on her chest.

'Don't touch me,' Emily said under her breath.

Godfrey smiled and backed away. 'What brings such an angel here? You accompany a Turk, yet your colour suggests that you are a Christian, and one who has not toiled in the sun. Even those with the purest of white skin have found themselves sullied by this devilish climate. How has one such as you maintained her pallor in this place? Which prince sent you here?'

'Sir,' the boy piped up before Emily could reply, 'she was with the heathen. I don't believe she is one of us. Look at her clothes. I think she came from the city too.'

Godfrey nodded, and Emily shuddered as he ran his fingers through her hair. 'Your clothing is strange; it seems you have been brought from distant lands. My, my, your captors really are devils, aren't they?' He sighed and shook his head. 'No doubt they have had you locked up in some dungeon where narry a ray of sunlight could reach your fair skin?'

He looked up at Lechasseur. 'Perhaps you have come to return her,' he said in a mocking tone, 'as some kind of "peace" offering?'

Godfrey's companions chuckled to themselves at this, but snapped quiet as their leader shot them a cold glance.

'We are travellers,' Lechasseur began. He stopped and looked around at the expectant faces. 'She is not a prisoner. We come not from this city, but from one far away. We're merchants. We heard about your struggle and we wanted to help, perhaps to trade supplies.'

'And what do you have to offer?' the loud man asked, looking intrigued.

'We can negotiate with the city authorities. Get you all the supplies you need. And in return, all we ask is that you give us information on the whereabouts of one of your number, who we believe poses a great danger to all our peoples.'

Emily was impressed by Lechasseur's charade. The natives seemed to be falling for it.

Godfrey looked puzzled, then burst out laughing with a great guffaw. 'So, you think that Godfrey de Bouillion is an easy target, eh? I know what you want, Saracen. You want us to remove the dams from your well streams, to allow your people access to the harvests outside the city. I can assure you we do not bargain with devils or their worshippers.'

Lechasseur managed to maintain his composure. 'We do not worship devils, I assure you.'

'You come from Antioch, where the Emir kills Christian children for pleasure, and expect me to believe that? Or are you one of the rare few; one who, despite holding the look of Lucifer in your eyes, has recanted and pledged his life to Christ?'

Emily knew from history books she had read at Honoré's flat that Antioch was the old name for somewhere in modern Turkey, but she couldn't remember exactly where. She could however remember that it had been the site of many great battles and much bloodshed. She realised that these people must be the Christian warriors that history would later come to call crusaders.

'I ... I am a Christian,' Lechasseur said. 'I wish only to see peace for all people, and it breaks my heart to see Christ's soldiers suffering in such conditions.'

Godfrey moved closer to Lechasseur and leaned forward until there was barely six inches separating their faces. 'I don't trust you, outsider. But if you have come from the city to betray your people, you may yet prove to be useful to me. Our siege will break the people of Antioch. God is with us. But you may be able to assist in the Lord's work.'

The man turned to his followers. 'He will not die today,' he announced. 'But if these strangers try any trickery or witchcraft, we will kill them instantly.'

Their conversation was interrupted as an out-of-breath young man entered the tent and hurried towards Godfrey.

'Sir!' he said, before quickly remembering his manners and giving a quick bow. 'It's happened again, sir.'

Godfrey leaned forward, his eyebrows arching. 'Another murder?'

The newcomer nodded. 'One of the tailors, sir. It is just like the others. His corpse is pale and desiccated, his face petrified with fear.' The man crossed himself. 'It is the Devil's work, sir.'

Godfrey frowned. 'And there is no evidence of a fight? No-one's admitting an honourable killing?'

The man shook his head. 'It must be the Saracen, sir. They are ungodly cowards. They don't proclaim their victories like we do.'

Godfrey stood up and turned to one of his entourage, a slender man in his late twenties with long blond hair, perfectly smooth skin and wearing a smart tunic, knee length boots and neatly cut hair, a man who seemed to be of a fairly high rank. 'Your thoughts, Simon?'

Simon shrugged. 'I don't think it's the Saracen. There's no evidence of their usual raiding tactics. Besides, we know they're primal, animalistic creatures who would not know to cover their tracks. The murderer must be someone closer. Or a stranger.'

Godfrey turned towards Emily and Lechasseur. 'Yes,' he said, his face baring teeth. 'A stranger ... Take them away.'

Simon and one of Godfrey's guards grabbed hold of Emily and Lechasseur and began to march them from the tent. Lechasseur started struggling but soon seemed to think better of it, deciding to go along with whatever they had in mind for now.

Emily had no intention of being so compliant. She wriggled in Simon's grasp, trying to break free. 'Wait!' she shouted. 'We can help you. Leave me alone!' She saw Lechasseur turn to her, his expression a silent plea for her to be quiet, but she wasn't having any of it. As her friend was led away and out of sight, she hoped he would be safe, and decided to raise the stakes. She kicked Simon hard on the shin and he recoiled, although he continued to hold her firmly in his grip.

'Simon?' Godfrey called over, clearly tiring of all the fuss. 'Send her to be a washerwoman. Now that most of our womenfolk have returned home to England, we could do with a few more servant girls.'

As Simon continued wrestling Emily toward the exit, she turned round and swung a punch at him, which he caught with his other hand. 'My, you are an aggressive one, aren't you!' he said.

'Get off me!' Emily cried.

'Don't worry, sir,' one of the other guards said, 'she is a lady, even if she has the disposition of an angry Turk! Maybe you can tame her for your pleasure.'

The room guffawed, relishing the spectacle. Emily didn't want to spend a moment longer with these primates. She slammed her elbow back into Simon's stomach. This time, she managed to wrench herself free from his grip, then tried to make her way out of the tent, but a row of guards with sworded belts around their waists had formed to block her path.

'You're a slave now, girl,' said Godfrey through gritted teeth, 'so behave like one – or face death.'

The guards advanced on Emily, the lead one drawing his sword. Emily waited until the last moment before ducking down and knocking him off balance. His sword clattered to the floor. More nimble than the knights, Emily managed to snatch up the weapon. Simon's reactions were also quick. 'I'll handle this!' he said to the other knights, drawing his own sword. Emily regained her balance, then lifted her sword to make contact with Simon's.

'Stop this stupidity!' Simon urged, but Emily was determined. She attempted to slice a blow into Simon's side, but he dodged it effectively, parrying back and almost hitting the girl. She was amazed she had actually avoided the blow. She'd fenced once or twice with Honoré, but this was a very different matter. The swords were about fifty times heavier than rapiers for a start, but adrenalin managed to keep Emily fighting. She dodged a few more blows, then managed to clip Simon. He looked down, shocked, clutched the wound and held his hand up. 'She drew blood!' he said, amazed.

Emily leaned forward, holding her sword to Simon's neck. 'Let me go free,' she said.

Emily sensed the other guards creeping up behind her. She turned to face them, but one managed to grab her sword arm and wrench the weapon out of it.

'Leave her!' Simon said, catching his breath. He turned to Godfrey. 'My Lord, the wench has spirit. I would like to request that she be my personal slave.'

Godfrey chuckled. 'Indeed she does put on a fair sport.' He gestured to the tent exit. 'You may take her away.'

The guards relaxed, groaning with disappointment as they resheathed their swords.

'I'm not your slave!' Emily insisted, glaring at Simon.

'Relax,' he whispered in her ear, still clutching the cut in his side. 'If you want to kill me, then you can do so in my tent. Making a fuss here will only result in your beheading.'

Now unarmed, Emily realised she had little choice but to go along with Simon's wishes. At least without the guards after her, she might get a chance to run away once they were outside.

The sun was beginning to set as Lechasseur was roughly pushed down into one of the pits in the ground that formed the crusaders' prison cells. He hoped that Emily was being treated a little better, wherever she was – though he rather doubted it.

In one corner of the pit, a bony figure with an Arabic complexion was urinating onto the ground. In another, a small child chewed ferociously on a piece of fruit that had clearly gone rotten many days ago, while rats scuttled around her. Honoré had thought the crusader camp to be the worst-smelling environment it was possible for anyone to experience, but the evil odour in this cell proved otherwise.

He cursed himself for having misjudged the situation so badly. How could he have been so naïve as to suppose that he and Emily could simply waltz into this unfamiliar historical period, in a distant foreign land, and talk the locals into revealing the whereabouts of the strange knight they had encountered in London? They didn't even know the knight's name, for heaven's sake! How had he let Emily talk him into embarking on this foolhardy endeavour in the first place? Maybe some of her adventurous spirit was rubbing off on him …

He looked up to the top of the pit and saw a guard standing at the edge of it, making sure no-one attempted to climb out. How long would he be kept here? He had no way of knowing; and it was hardly reassuring to think that if and when he was released, he would still be suspected of treachery, and possibly even murder. He decided he was going to have to try tactics that were a little more forceful if he didn't want to end up spending the foreseeable future down here with the rats.

He cracked his knuckles and loosened his joints before reaching up towards the guard's legs. This was going to be an interesting night.

4

Emily sat staring at the scrawny carcass of a pig roasting on a spit over a fire that had been lit outside Simon's tent. It was dark now, yet still one of Simon's squires was guarding over her, as he had been for the last few hours, making sure that she didn't try to get away. Simon himself stood beside Emily, waiting for the pig to finish cooking.

Emily was sure she could hear a distant wolf howl, or was it a growl? Either way, running into the desert was something even she wasn't reckless enough to try.

'You know I won't run away,' Emily told her captor bluntly. 'At least not until morning.'

Simon smiled and looked up at the squire. 'At ease, Aethelred. Join us at the fire.' The man took one more suspicious look at Emily, then moved to sit down next to his captive, shoulders relaxing as he did so.

'Emily,' Simon said, 'I want you to be happy here. You'll never survive on your own, not if that murdering Saracen you consorted with has been punished for his sins. You can make this much easier on yourself. Try to see the good in the situation in which you find yourself. Taking the cross is a wonderful thing indeed. Please don't listen to the Devil. Please fight it.'

Emily closed her eyes and felt the heat of the flickering fire gently warming her eyelids. She imagined she was back home, sitting by the fire in Honoré's flat in London, or in some country hotel away from the bustle of the city. But when she opened her eyes again, her daydreams shattered as she found herself back in this hot, unpleasant and hazardous environment. It wasn't just the terrible smells that upset her, or the degrading way in which, as a woman, she was treated, but more being so very far away from anything resembling

25

familiarity or home comforts.

She and Honoré had travelled into the past and into the future, had seen wondrous possibilities and probabilities, but this was the first time they had travelled into distant history, the first time she had felt quite so anachronistic and out of place. This was not just a different culture, a different time period, but a totally unfamiliar way of living.

Emily had never met royalty before. While princes like Godfrey were far from her idea of refinement, the way they'd constructed mini-courts, complete with followers at all levels, even slaves, in spite of the heat and lack of resources, was an impressive show of how tightly knit the feudal system was. It was a strange set up, and one that Emily found it very uncomfortable to be a part of. Faith was at the centre of everyone's lives here. Everything revolved around it. I can't even remember who I really am, Emily thought. How am I supposed to know if I've sinned or not? There were just so many loopholes, so many contradictions. Yet for these people, religion was the only reason they had to live. After all, it was only the promise of a better afterlife that kept them going through such squalor and suffering. If only that afterlife didn't have to come with spilling the blood of innocents too. Emily had never met anyone who talked about God more than these people, yet for all the talk of Christ and of doing the Pope's work, they wouldn't think twice about beheading or stabbing an enemy, or even a fellow soldier who betrayed them. It was a lawless and dangerous place, and she knew Honoré would face worse treatment than most here.

Miles away from any authority, the princes in charge of the crusade acted like children let out without their parents, heedless of all sense of responsibility and morals. It was no surprise that their men followed their lead and soon abandoned all pretence of civility. The whole camp had hanging over it the oppressive air of an explosion waiting to happen.

Simon had explained that the princes' contingents had been waiting outside the city for six months now, tired, hungry and hot, with little to occupy them but short raids and occasional skirmishes. In an effort to starve the people of Antioch out of their besieged city, the crusading armies had blocked all the supply routes and made sure that any food deliveries were met with the sort of bloodthirsty hospitality their forces had become notorious for. Emily knew that things couldn't stay like this for much longer.

'How long do you think it will be before Antioch falls?' she asked.

Simon shrugged. 'It depends. We underestimated their stock, clearly. We've dammed their waterways, killed any outsiders who've tried to trade with them, and raided the outskirts enough times for them to know we are powerful, but still they resist.'

'Wouldn't it be easier just to march in and take the city?'

This time Aethelred laughed, burping as he did so before wiping his mouth on his arm. 'Wench, look at us,' he snapped. 'Do you know how many years we've toiled to get here? If we mounted a full scale attack, we would be massacred trying to get through the walls. Even if we took the city, we don't have enough men to make it to Jerusalem, not without waiting for more pilgrims to arrive. Besides, we have tried. Many times. But they have too many soldiers, and their walls are too strong.'

Simon's face was cold. 'Six months ago,' he began, 'the Turks sent an army from Damascus to destroy us.'

'It was a great victory for Christ,' Aethelred chipped in.

Simon shook his head. 'My uncle led the battle against them, flanked by Lord Bohemond's men. It was a terrible day for Christ's pilgrims. Although we killed or enslaved every one of the Turkish horde, the dead were many on our side. As Heaven fills with the fallen soldiers, our hearts grow emptier. That time took a lot out of us, and taught us to be careful.'

'But we are not cowards,' Aethelred said. 'We should be the ones in charge. We should take the city from the Turks before we too starve.'

'We wait,' Simon continued, 'because we have to. Because

27

it's all we can do.' He took a sip from his flagon. Emily wondered if its contents explained his candour.

'Why are you telling me this?' she asked.

Simon stood up and stretched. 'If you knew what we've been through, if you knew how noble our cause was ...' He reached across and took Emily's hand in his, but she snatched it away. 'We mean no harm,' he continued. 'We're just doing God's work. Do not fight the tide, Emily.'

Emily folded her arms, a gesture of defiance. 'Do I have much choice?'

Simon knelt down, his voice a whisper. 'Emily, there are few women in the camp. We sent them all home as conditions deteriorated. That means you are a sought-after prize, and constantly need to be on your guard for those who might take advantage of you. Serve me well and I will not only protect you from their advances but also ensure a great life for you when we reach Jerusalem, or here if you prefer to stay in this city. A far greater life than you could have had with that merchant.'

The fire began to spark as it burned down. Emily knew it was futile to continue her protests. 'I'm going to bed,' she said. She was worried Simon would take this as an invitation, but he simply smiled and stood back. 'You'll meet the other girls,' he said, pointing to the washerwomen's tent. 'If they give you trouble, just ask me for help.'

Emily thanked Simon and moved toward the tent, almost impressed by his chivalry. Perhaps there was hope for some of these knights yet.

Emily cautiously peered inside. She saw a group of women getting ready to go to sleep, and felt envious. Being so far from home, not knowing whether Honoré was alive or dead, and surrounded by such squalor, she wanted nothing more than to curl up in a comfy bed and forget about everything, but she knew she had to keep awake and strong, for Honoré's sake.

Emily introduced herself to the other girls who seemed friendly enough. A small comfort. One young woman, Edith, had a tiny baby that seemed to take an instant liking to Emily.

'William likes you,' Edith said with surprise. 'He normally cries around strangers.'

'Perhaps she'll fit in well here,' an old lady with a kindly face said. A brief bout of small-talk ensued, though Emily was pleased that the residents of the tent did not seem too nosy. There were a few questions about how she came into Simon's service and why they had not seen her before, but for the most part the interrogation was light. The girls ranged in ages from one barely older than seven, to the old woman, Cecily, who admitted that she was probably going to be taking the short cut to the Land of Milk and Honey rather than be able to march all the way to Jerusalem.

Cecily reached into a wicker basket and pulled out a pile of clothes, which she handed to Emily. 'Here, take these. Change into something a bit more Christian.'

Emily gladly took the clothes, and put on a medieval dress over her 20th Century undergarments. The new dress was itchy and uncomfortable, but far lighter than her old one, and she was relieved to be wearing something cooler at last. The new dress went all the way down to her ankles, which was impractical, but would at least stop the men leering at her legs.

'Come on,' Edith called over as Emily finished changing, 'you'd better get some sleep. We've a lot to be getting on with tomorrow.'

'I can't sleep,' Emily confided. 'You have to help me get out of here. I need to find my friend, Honoré. He's been taken away, arrested.'

Cecily looked intrigued. 'Another newcomer, is he? Why's he been arrested? What's he been up to?'

'He hasn't done anything wrong,' Emily insisted. 'We just came here to look for someone. A knight.'

The woman snorted. 'There are plenty of knights here. Did you want any one in particular?'

'I … I'm not sure. Where would they have taken my friend?'

Edith now chipped in. 'If Lord Godfrey has not handed him to one of the other princes, then they'll have thrown him in the pits.' She gestured to one side. 'Keep following the camp that way, you'll soon find them.'

'Who are these other princes?' Emily asked.

The woman looked surprised. 'Our armies come from all over Europe, each one under a different prince's command. It's only by uniting side-by-side that we have enough men to flank this cursed city. You would be wise to examine the pits, though. If your friend was handed to one of the other Lords, he may already be dead.'

Emily thanked the ladies and moved to the exit.

'You're not going now, are you?' Cecily rasped. 'It's dangerous in the dark.'

'I'll take my chances,' Emily said.

The woman shrugged. 'And where do you intend to go once you've found him? There's nowhere for miles around, except the city. The Turks will slaughter you before you get near them.'

Emily shook her head. 'At least I'll be able to free my friend. He's no criminal. It's only because he's black that they're suspicious of him.'

Edith laughed harshly. 'A Saracen? No wonder they arrested him. He may have a Frankish name, but appearances don't lie in a place like this.'

'He's not a Saracen. We're just traders. We told them that.'

Cecily sniffed to indicate her disapproval. 'You ought to think whether the Lord might consider consorting with such creatures as blasphemy, you know. I doubt the Pope would approve.'

Emily was about to make some comment about the Pope taking a running jump, but decided against it.

'I have to try to rescue him. As a white girl, I should at least escape being killed for being a Saracen.'

Cecily smiled again. 'Child, you really don't know our masters at all, do you?'

Emily peered around the canvas flap at the front of the

washerwomen's tent and crept into the darkness outside. She moved around the different tents trying to get her bearings and match her location to Cecily's directions. The camp was difficult to navigate. All the tents were similar, with only the coats of arms painted on the front distinguishing them, as the different families from across France, Normandy, England and many smaller European principalities staked their claim on territory that they prayed history would bestow on them, the right to own it divinely given to them alone.

Eventually Emily found her way to the holding cells. Little more than a row of pits, the place smelled even worse than the rest of the camp, something Emily really hadn't thought possible.

She peered into the first pit in the row. 'Honoré!' she hissed. 'Honoré!'

Silence. 'Can you hear me?'

A hand clamped on to her shoulder and she spun around in shock.

'You are not to see the prisoners,' the guard informed her. 'Unless you want to join them.'

Emily scowled. 'Please, just let me have a few words with the Saracen man who arrived today.'

The guard shook his head. 'No-one talks to the prisoners.'

Emily decided to try to take the high ground. 'Just wait until Lord Godfrey hears of this,' she stormed, and tried to pass the guard.

He pushed Emily away from him and she lost her balance, her foot skidding over the edge of the pit. The guard chuckled to himself as Emily fell into the dark hole, tumbling down the side to the bottom.

Emily sat in pitch darkness, feeling very foolish. After a moment, a deep and familiar hot chocolate voice said, 'What sort of a scrape have you got yourself into this time, then?'

Emily tenderly picked herself up off the ground and hobbled over to the man-shaped shadow standing there.

'I was worried they'd killed you,' she said, giving Honoré a hug. He winced as she did so, evidently sore around the ribs.

JON DE BURGH MILLER

'Sometimes,' he replied, 'I wish they had. They're not ones to be messed with, you know.'

'Hey!' Emily shouted up to the guard. 'Get me out of here!' She heard mocking laughter coming from above the pit. 'This isn't funny!'

'Quiet, wench!' the guard called. 'You wanted to see your friend ... so see him.'

Emily sighed. She was tired and needed sleep, but knew there was no way she could bear to even shut her eyes in this place. In the end, she nodded off resting in Honoré's arms, as he stayed alert to anyone who might try and approach them in the night.

5

As dawn broke, the crusader camp became a hive of activity. While Lechasseur was made to wait in the pit, Emily was hauled out by a pair of guards and taken to Godfrey's tent. On the way, she passed several crowds of men busy at work hammering pieces of wood and metal, while others planned out military tactics with rocks and badges laid out on tables. There was an excited buzz in the air. Something of great importance was clearly about to happen. Emily wondered if this was the day that the crusaders would finally make their push toward the city.

She found Godfrey slouched in front of a slab of stone that was serving as a table, nibbling on a pathetic looking bit of meat. From his frown, Emily guessed he was used to rather more generous fare than the crusaders were able to scrape together after months of besieging the city.

'Sit down, girl!' Godfrey said, rising from his makeshift table. 'We wouldn't want you attempting to kill me now, would we?

'I didn't kill anyone,' Emily said, before planting herself on a bale of straw next to the table. 'And neither did Honoré.' The seat itched and Emily had to wriggle around to get comfortable. It was a sight Godfrey that clearly found amusing, but his humour only made Emily more irritated.

'As I'm sure you've heard, several of our men – good men, good Christian men – have been killed in their sleep by cowards who refuse to admit their crimes.' He gestured toward one of his guards. 'I have these men to keep me safe, of course, but most of Christ's soldiers aren't so lucky.' He looked at Emily and did his best to stare piercingly into her eyes. 'And coincidentally, you arrive from nowhere, just as another murder befalls us. Accompanied by a Saracen.'

Emily sighed. 'Look, I know my friend and I don't exactly fit in around here, but do you really think we'd be so obvious about it if we were murderers?'

'You are a woman,' Godfrey said with a chuckle. 'Not exactly known for using your head!'

Emily didn't find the joke funny, unlike Godfrey's guards, who gave sycophantic false belly laughs.

Emily realised she was going to have to demonstrate some form of ability that would gain her respect from her captors. 'May I see one of the bodies?' she asked. 'I have some knowledge of medicine, healing and human anatomy. I may be able to find something that will lead us to the real murderer.'

Godfrey looked at Emily with outright incredulity. 'And what would a wench like you know of such things? Matters of life and death are the province of our Lord.'

'Sir,' one of the guards said, 'she was in the company of a Saracen. They may practice witchcraft the likes of which we could never imagine. Perhaps they can put a curse on the murderer, save any more of us from being taken from our quest?'

Godfrey walked over to Emily and looked into her face, seeking any sign of a trick. She shivered, and Godfrey turned to his vassals. 'I suppose it can do no harm. Besides, I'd like to know how she copes with the sight of one of *those* corpses! Find Turstin's body, and let her take a look. Just make sure she refrains from touching anything she should not.' He turned back to Emily. 'I'll be back by Terce, and I expect to be told the results of your wicked practices.'

The dead had been laid out in a row on the outskirts of the camp in a naturally occurring ditch. Despite Godfrey's words about matters of life and death being reserved for God, there had been little attempt to cover the bodies – in times of such hardship, no-one could afford to waste a skin or a cloth on a corpse – and they'd been dumped to be eaten by the vultures, flies and wild dogs that occasionally scrabbled around the area looking for food. A few shovels of sand had been used to cover them and try to stop the stench from spreading, but most of it had blown away, the soil being too light and the work too much effort for the crusaders to persist with.

Godfrey had sent one of his vassals to accompany Emily, along with a burly guard to make sure she didn't try to escape. The vassal reached down into the ditch and yanked one of the corpses up towards them. The other bodies tumbled to the side as their companion was removed. As the guard held the corpse up, Emily found herself inches away from the rictus grinning face of a man who had obviously been terrified in his final moments.

The vassal threw the body down to the ground beside the ditch, and Emily crouched to examine it, trying not to be fazed by the gruesome sight. Unlike most people of this era, she had rarely seen death in the flesh before (at least, not in the part of her life that she remembered …), and every time she was confronted by it she felt a chill inside, as if part of her was nagging her to get away, not to get to involved, while another part was fascinated by the spectacle.

The body was a pale, off-white shade, battered and bruised, perhaps from years of fighting, and clad in rags. In places, Emily noted, its flesh was starting to decompose.

'Do your work,' the vassal said, 'but you do not have long.'

'Do you know how they died?' Emily asked.

'They were all stabbed in the neck.'

Taking a deep breath and trying not to think of the germs she must be picking up by touching the body, Emily turned the corpse over with her foot to look at the back of the head. A clear, star-shaped wound was visible at the base of the neck, from which a thin line of black-clotted blood ran to the shoulder blades.

'It looks almost as if they've been killed for their blood, or at least something inside them …'

The vassal raised an eyebrow.

'Look at this,' Emily continued. 'The wound has bruising

around it, which suggests that something was inserted here. Do they all have a mark like this?'

The vassal nodded silently, and Emily turned to address him. 'I didn't kill them, you know. Neither Honoré nor I even have weapons, let alone something that could make a wound like that.'

The vassal shrugged. 'That's for Lord Godfrey to decide.'

Emily stood outside Simon's tent for almost a minute, trying to summon up as much resolve and courage as she could, before finally she cleared her throat and marched inside. Simon stood in the middle of the room with his arms outstretched while one of his squires struggled to attach an awkward and heavy-looking plate of armour to his chest.

'Emily,' Simon said. 'So the wolves didn't get you?'

She marched over. 'Listen Simon, I've seen the bodies of the dead soldiers, and I think I know why they were killed.'

The squire stopped, his eyes widening, before Simon motioned for him to continue.

'Go on.'

'I believe someone is extracting substances from inside the bodies, harvesting something specific rather than just killing out of cold malice.'

Emily explained the mark she had seen on the corpse's neck. Simon seemed unconcerned. 'It matters little why they died,' he said. 'What matters is who the killer is.'

'But the clues can help us, don't you see? Who would want to drain fluid from the body?'

'The devils of course. So it was a Saracen?'

'I don't think so,' Emily said, still not quite sure of herself but playing along. 'I didn't sense any … erm … devils. They didn't leave any of the marks we know they normally do.'

Simon looked slightly bemused, and Emily realised she was perhaps over-egging things. She had to play the situation to her advantage, to use her alleged expertise to get back to Honoré and find the mysterious knight.

'I think the killer is the same man my friend and I are here looking for. I haven't seen him around so far, but he definitely came from here.'

'Describe him,' Simon said, intrigued.

'An elderly man, though quite strong. Still a fighter.'

'There are many old fighters here. Why, Lord Godfrey himself would fit the description.'

'You should have seen his face,' Emily continued. 'As white as a sheet, with a beard down to here,' she put her hands on her waist, 'and hair that was pretty much falling out.'

Simon shook his head. 'I do not believe we have anyone here of that description. Tell me, where did you see this man?'

'In another city.' Emily neglected to mention that it was also in another century. 'He owed Honoré a great deal of money, and we need to speak to him urgently.'

Simon laughed. 'You mean your friend intends to exact vengeance? An honourable goal, indeed. If I see someone like that, I will be sure to tell him to find you.'

Emily wondered if the mysterious knight was using his apparent time-travelling abilities on a more localised scale. Honoré had said that he didn't seem to have touched other time periods apart from the one they were in now and 1950. Emily wondered how to describe time travel to a medieval knight. 'Simon,' she asked, 'has there been anything strange occurring? Perhaps someone appearing from the air,' she struggled to think of the words. 'Like our Lord Jesus Christ, descending from Heaven. Has there been anyone who has seemed to be in two places at once?'

The squire, who had remained quiet until now, put down the remaining items of armour. 'Who is this strange woman, master?' His eyes gleamed as he looked at Emily. 'With your permission, master, I might like to marry her one day.'

Simon stared at Emily with a look that told her to be quiet but Emily was quickly learning the best ways to get results among medieval knights. 'At the moment, I have more pressing concerns,' she said calmly. 'The will of God must be enacted. I come from a convent to help the Lord's people through these hard times.'

The squire seemed impressed. Thankfully Simon said nothing to refute her story.

Simon changed the subject. 'I suppose,' he began, 'there has been one strange occurrence.'

The squire looked up at his master in puzzlement. 'Master?'

Simon looked at the squire and smiled. 'I think we should introduce her to Alice.'

Simon said little about the person they were going to see as he walked with Emily to the far end of the camp. What they found was an old woman crouched over a cooking pot, trying to light a fire to boil some water.

'Hello Alice,' Simon said, bowing his head to the old woman. 'This is Emily of Blandish, a spiritual woman with knowledge that belies her appearance. She would like to know more about what you saw.'

The old woman squinted at the newcomers. She turned away from them and sat down by the animal skins she had been sewing into blankets.

Emily stepped closer to the old woman. 'Please Alice,' she said gently. 'Is it true you had a vision?'

Alice picked up a needle and began to stitch the skins together. 'There are people in this camp who say terrible, blasphemous things about the Pope's words. Terrible, heartbreaking things.'

Emily reached out and touched Alice's shoulder. 'What have they been saying?'

'That all this, all we've been through, all those children dying and suffering ... that it is all for nothing, that we are not the chosen people of our Lord, that there is no paradise waiting for us in Jerusalem.' Her voice rose, angry. 'They're wrong, girl. I've seen it. I saw Saint Luke appear to me, down by the well, as I was fetching water. He rose from the sea and told me I was blessed.'

'What did the Saint look like?'

'A knight to equal the best of the men here, but with a halo of light, a blue fire, and the feeling of death, a chill that ran through my bones. I knew that what I saw was not of this Earth.'

'Tell me,' said Emily, 'did the Saint remind you of anyone you've met here?'

The woman shook her head. 'My head was bowed in duty. I did not take time to examine him closely.' The woman was getting irritated. 'Now, if you please.'

Emily nodded. 'Thank you for your time.'

As they left the old woman's tent, Emily turned to Simon. 'I don't know, I mean I can't be sure, but I think that might have been our man that she saw. If he can time- ... I don't know. I need to talk to Honoré.'

Simon held Emily's shoulder and turned her around until her face was close to his. 'Emily, please,' he said. 'Can't we just enjoy some time together? Relax a little. It makes such a change to have such intelligent company.'

'Simon,' Emily began, 'I'm sorry. It's just that ... I must find Honoré.'

Simon nodded. 'I have been thinking about your problem. It is possible that the Bishop of Le Puy may be able to help you find the man you seek. I will arrange an audience with him for when you return.

'Thanks,' Emily muttered, before walking away from Simon, leaving him standing in her wake, wondering what he had said to cause such a cold reaction from her.

6

'Saracen!'

Honoré Lechasseur was jolted awake by the shout.

'Get up, Saracen!'

Lechasseur blinked away the grime around his eyes and looked up at the guard. Finally he was getting out of this hole. He yawned, then hitched himself off the floor, reaching his arms up towards the guards. There were two of them this time, and they reached down and hauled him out. As he found his balance, one of the guards withdrew his sword from its sheath, making it clear that Lechasseur wasn't to try anything.

He turned to see Emily, arms folded, a large grin on her face. 'I told you I'd convince them you were innocent,' she said.

'You are free to go, on order of Simon of Lorraine.'

Lechasseur turned to the guards. 'Thanks,' he said, making the gesture of tipping a hat.

He and Emily began to walk away, in the direction of Simon's tent. As they did so, Emily filled him in on what she'd learned, and retold the old crone's tale.

'She's not the only one seeing things,' Lechasseur revealed. 'I overheard the guards talking. Lots of people are seeing things. Visions, Saints ... you know.'

'Time travelling knights?'

Lechasseur smirked. 'Time travelling Saracens.'

There was a brief silence before Emily continued. 'Don't let them get to you,' she said. 'You know you're better than them, that you're not what they say you are.'

Lechasseur grinned at her. 'So what have you found?'

'We keep trying.' Emily said. 'Simon says that the foragers see people coming and going from the camp the whole time. Perhaps –'

'Emily,' Lechasseur interrupted. 'This Simon guy ...'

Now it was Emily's turn to raise an eyebrow. 'Not jealous are we?' she joked.

Lechasseur snorted. 'Be careful, Emily. You can't trust these people.'

Emily shook her head. 'He's been good to me. After a bad start, admittedly. I think he really wants to help us, you know.'

'I know what he wants.'

Emily snorted at Lechasseur's awkwardness. 'I'm a big girl, I can look after myself.'

Lechasseur sighed. 'I know. That's not what I mean. This isn't the fifties, you know. These crusaders ... they don't respect women, they're not gentlemen.'

'I beat him in a sword-fight.'

Lechasseur looked impressed. 'Just be careful, okay? We stick out like a dislocated shoulder here, yet this guy switches from wanting us dead to wanting to risk his safety to help us. I just think there's something not right here.'

Emily shook her head and smiled. 'You're crazy, you know? But thanks for the concern. And I promise, I'll be careful.'

Lechasseur nodded. 'Where to now, then?' he asked.

'Simon's managed to arrange for us to meet someone very interesting. It'll be getting dark soon, so we'd better get a move on.'

Adhemar of Le Puy was the most important representative of the Church in the whole camp, and a relatively young bishop. When word had reached the Vatican of the disaster of the People's journey from Claremont, the Pope had feared that the Normans would make an even worse job of things, and so had decided to send the lowliest and least proven of his bishops to sort them out. A controversial man, alleged to have witnessed a miracle, Adhemar had also become something of a liability to the Church in Rome – a fact not entirely unrelated to his selection for this new role. The crusade allowed the Church to solve many of its problems.

A large knight armed with an equally large sword, partially rusted yet still deadly, stood between the Bishop and his visitors.

Adhemar cleared his throat. 'Godfrey assures me you are not here to assassinate Christ's envoy, so I will let you speak your mind.'

Lechasseur nodded. 'We come from afar, looking for a criminal who stole something of great value to us. He was last seen dressed in Norman armour. He was elderly, about so tall, with a long white beard and eyes of fire.'

Adhemar shrugged. 'And why do you come to me? Do you believe the faith of Christ will help you in your search?'

Lechasseur cleared his throat. 'We are already Christians, sir, but we have heard that you have seen many strange things in the last few weeks.'

Adhemar sighed. 'All is not well with the Christian Church. The Lord Almighty is suffering as his holy city is ransacked by the Turks.'

'Well,' Emily said, 'with God on our side, victory will soon be ours.' She looked over at Lechasseur for support. He looked impressed and nodded for her to continue. 'And once it is, we shall restore Jerusalem to a state greater than it has been since the day Our Lord himself was crucified.'

Adhemar nodded, eyebrows raised in surprise at her words. He waved his guard closer, at the same time beckoning for Lechasseur and Emily to move nearer.

'The dead walk among us. They will us on to victory. The Holy Spirit is in evidence, giving us the strength we need to fulfil our pilgrimage.' He leaned towards Lechasseur, his voice a harsh whisper. 'I've seen the spirits of the dead; several I recognised as among those we have lost in battle. Death is everywhere in this city of evil, and suffering. I've seen these apparitions travel between here and the city, and they are not alone. Minions of Lucifer are watching, waiting, trying to blend in with us unnoticed.'

'And do any of these minions look like old men in armour,

with long white beards?'

Adhemar seemed confused by Honoré's question and shook his head, then turned to wave them away.

'They all come from the city, sooner or later,' he said. 'It's held by devils, and the hardest place yet to fall to pilgrim hands. If the man you seek is anywhere to be found in this unholy land, it will be in Antioch.'

Lechasseur thanked the Bishop for his time, and he and Emily turned to leave the tent.

'One more thing,' Adhemar called after them. 'Be on your guard. As newcomers, you may be seen by the devils as more susceptible to temptation than most, so be mindful of their presence. The armies of Lucifer are nothing if not opportunistic.'

'Thanks for your advice,' Lechasseur said. 'We'll be careful.'

As Emily and Lechasseur left the Bishop's tent, Adhemar turned to his guard. 'I fear those two will not live to see us reach our goal,' he sighed. 'May the Lord have mercy on their souls.'

'So where next?' a weary Emily asked as she and Lechasseur sat on cushions inside Simon's tent. Lechasseur looked into the middle distance. 'When I saw the knight's time snake,' he reflected, 'it led us to this camp. Given his skin colouring and armour, he's clearly a European. But maybe the Bishop's right, and he is somewhere in the city. He might be a dissident, or a deserter from the crusaders' forces –'

His words were interrupted by a terrified scream coming from outside. Everyone in the tent seemed to stand up at once. Emily and Lechasseur looked at each other, then hurried across to the entrance.

Lechasseur faltered on the threshold as his legs seemed to turn to jelly, and then to stop responding completely. A strange paralysis seemed to overtake him, spreading from his legs and up his whole body.

He looked over at Emily and the others in the tent. They too were struggling as if trapped in quicksand, with confused expressions on their faces. 'What the –'

Lechasseur tried to reach down to feel his legs, but found that his entire body was frozen. He felt like an insect swimming through fast-hardening amber.

'What's happening to us?' Emily managed to say, but her words slurred as the paralysis took hold.

Another scream came from outside, then was silenced, replaced by a sliding and slurping noise, not unlike a stomach rumbling but amplified and distorted many times over.

The noise eventually died away. Emily and Lechasseur continued to struggle, and in a few seconds found that they were once again able to move.

'What just happened?' Emily asked.

Lechasseur breathed a heavy sigh. 'Let's find out.'

He moved to the entrance to the tent and lifted the flap. In the flickering shadows outside, he saw what appeared to be a large, serpentine shape moving rapidly away from a fallen body. As he approached the body, he saw that the killer had struck again, leaving a dead husk of a man, face contorted in a rictus scream, patches of decomposition already creeping across the skin of the face.

Emily and Simon, along with several vassals, joined him by the body. Gasps of shock and terror rippled through the group.

Lechasseur reached down and felt under the dead man's throat for a pulse. His fingers pushed through rotting skin and he withdrew them quickly. 'He's dead.'

A flash of light caught Lechasseur's eye. 'Hang on, what's this …' He removed a metal disc from beneath the man's arm.

'Oh God,' Emily said as she looked at the body. 'It's just like the other one. The decomposition, the look of fear on his face …'

'Emily!' Simon said. 'You should stay inside. It isn't safe. The murderer might still be nearby.' He gestured to two of the guards, and they picked up the body and moved it inside the tent.

As Simon escorted Emily back under cover, Lechasseur looked around. Somewhere in this camp was a killer … and going by the glimpse he had caught, it wasn't even remotely human.

By the light of several flaming torches, Simon and his advisors studied the metal disc Lechasseur had found. 'It's definitely a coin from the city,' one of the advisors said. 'The murderer must be a Saracen.'

'I don't know about that,' Lechasseur said dourly.

'And what would you propose we do to catch this murderer?' Simon asked.

Lechasseur had been thinking about this. 'I want you to help me arrange an expedition. Tomorrow night, I'm going into Antioch.'

Emily was taken aback. 'Honoré, are you mad? If they see you near the city ... both sides will probably have your head.'

Lechasseur smiled. 'Relax. I'll be fine.'

'It won't be easy,' Simon told them. 'Godfrey will never allow you to leave the camp. I may be charged with monitoring you, but you are still his prisoners.'

'Simon, Simon,' Lechasseur said, putting his arm around the knight's shoulder like an old friend. 'Just tell me the safest way to get inside the city, ask a couple of men to come with me, and tell everyone we're going to raid for food. We can keep the murder investigation side of things nice and quiet.'

Simon sighed. 'I suppose so.'

Emily jabbed Lechasseur in the ribs. 'What was it you said about staying away from Simon? I hope you agree now he has his uses.'

Simon scowled at her, but she could tell he had taken the joke in the spirit in which it was meant.

Lechasseur shrugged, reluctantly conceding Emily's point. 'I still think you should be careful.'

'He's right,' Simon said, misunderstanding. 'The city is a harsh place. You both should be sure you know what you are letting yourself in for.'

Lechasseur shrugged. 'I can handle myself.'

'He's right,' Emily said. 'We've been through a lot, you know, Simon.'

Simon took Emily by the arm and marched her out of earshot of Lechasseur.

'Look, Emily,' he whispered, 'I'm sure he can look after himself, but you don't seem to understand quite how dangerous this place is. Look around you – people are being injured and killed every day. Please, don't go to the city. Stay here.'

Emily was unsure what to make of this. 'Why do you care so much?'

Simon looked away. 'Emily, you have spirit, and I … I like you. You're confident and unafraid, and that's good, but I'm worried you will soon be killed after taking one too many chances.'

Emily was surprised at Simon's concern. Surely he had other things to worry about than her safety? But he seemed to be telling the truth.

'You did have me thrown in the prison pit,' she reminded him.

Simon smiled, embarrassed. 'I'm sorry. That was a misunderstanding. You're free to come and go as you please, you're not my slave. Just don't tell Godfrey I told you that.'

Lechasseur walked up behind them. 'So what's the plan?'

'Promise me you'll stay,' Simon urged Emily.

She nodded. 'Okay then, but just for this raid. The next time you go into the city, I'll be there.' She turned to Lechasseur. 'I'm going to look after things here, keep an eye out in case there are any more murders.'

'Everything you need should be ready by sundown tomorrow,' Simon informed Lechasseur. 'I'll have some people ready to accompany you.'

'Thanks,' Lechasseur said. He shook Simon's hand – the first time their skins had touched – and a momentary look of concern flashed across his face, before he grinned widely once more. He glanced at Emily and saw that she had noticed his reaction. She frowned at him, and he gave a quick shake of his head before moving over to the group of advisors. He asked them again about the coin, then shook hands with several of them as he took his leave.

When he had done, he escorted Emily out of the tent and off to a quiet area away from the throng of people.

'What was that all about?' she asked, once they were alone.

Lechasseur had a grave expression on his face. 'Something terrible is going to happen,' he whispered. 'Their time snakes aren't right. Simon's is like nothing I've ever seen before, and the others ... They're supposed to stretch on for many years, but they all seem to stop abruptly. Within the next few days. I don't know how to describe it ... It's like I can see the path their life is supposed to take, but the snake has been cut in two, terminated before its time.'

'But what does that mean?'

Lechasseur sighed. 'Emily, I think whatever our time travelling knight is doing, he's messing with history on such a level that thousands of people are going to die before their time because of him. Whoever he is, once we've found him, we have to stop him.'

Lechasseur spent the next day studying plans of the city, and talking to people who had been there before, to find the best way to move around undetected. Simon had assigned two of his vassals, Timothy and Edward, and a warrior preacher, a man named Peter, to accompany him on his foray. As Lechasseur watched the sun set, the small raiding party made its final preparations to infiltrate the city. The rumours he'd picked up from his fellow prisoners were that the crusaders never went near the city other than to attack in daylight, that their patience and ability to wait for months on end was what most worried the people of Antioch. But as he heard the chatter of Timothy and Edward, he realised that this was actually the latest in a long line of raids into the city. Simon had assured him that Antioch's military forces would be defending the main city gates and would not be bothered with three stragglers from the enemy camp, but he was still worried. They could be killed on sight. He was also concerned about having a preacher come with them, but the vassals seemed insistent that it was necessary to ensure God watched over and protected their expedition.

Timothy and Edward were young men from Flanders who, since moving into Simon's service, had established themselves as accomplished spies thanks to successfully making it past the city defences on three previous occasions. The omens looked as good as could be hoped for. Lechasseur wasn't exactly sure what he expected to find in the city, but he had strong suspicions that he was far more likely to find his prey there than outside the city walls. He hoped he would be able to find an excuse to separate from the others in order to conduct his search. He guessed that with his complexion he would be able to move about undetected, but it was still a risky operation. He had visions of everything going swimmingly, only for him to be killed by an arrow as he returned to the crusader camp, them seeing nothing but a dark face and not realising who he was. But one step at a time. First he had to find the old man.

'So how dangerous is this?' Lechasseur wondered as he struggled to insert a sword into a scabbard he had tied around his waist, before giving up and taking a large dagger instead.

'We must be careful,' Peter said. 'Two of our friends were lost to the devils last time we tried. Only we returned.'

Timothy gestured to the torch-lit camp behind them. 'Our people are starving, we have little choice. Antioch has been under siege for months now, but they must have more supplies than we realised. They would have capitulated by now otherwise. We have to take the chance, for the survival of our kinfolk.'

Edward grunted and gestured a thumb at Lechasseur. 'How do we know he won't betray us?'

Lechasseur raised a hand to calm the suspicious crusader. 'I know about bartering and trading for scarce items of food. Just give me the chance to get you some supplies, then you'll see I'm no threat to you.'

Timothy nodded enthusiastically. 'Simon tells us he's a merchant, Edward. If we encounter any difficulty, he may be able to deceive the Saracen into letting us leave with our quarry. I am tired of eating rats and thistles.'

'And I don't exactly look Norman either,' Lechasseur reminded them. The crusaders thought on this, then nodded, Edward's suspicions at least temporarily mollified.

Edward adjusted his chain mail poncho. The three crusaders wore minimal sets of armour, but Lechasseur preferred freedom of movement and so stuck to a leather tunic. He considered that the dagger would be useful for self-defence if it came to that.

'Come,' Timothy said. 'Let us depart.' He turned to Lechasseur and grinned. 'I look forward to seeing what bounty your wicked ways will bring us.'

7

The small group moved swiftly across the quarter of a mile or so that separated the encampment from the city walls. Although the terrain was rugged and tricky to navigate, Lechasseur's eyes adjusted quickly to the darkness and they made good time. Timothy explained that the only entrance to the city they could use without being spotted was a small gap in the walls left over from some long-forgotten attack, but as it was on the North face, it was a lengthy trek from the camp.

Lechasseur still felt uneasy, especially with Edward, who had made it clear he had little time for people of Lechasseur's colour.

'So you've been on this crusade a long time, then?' Lechasseur said, making conversation.

'We have suffered for almost two years now.' Peter's voice was laced with bitterness. 'This country is poisoned. It's hot, there's little water, even less food ...'

'It is the ultimate test of our righteousness,' interjected Timothy. 'The Lord dictated that each and every one of us leave our wives and families to help with the effort to liberate Jerusalem, but at each point along the way we have been faced with trials.'

'You left families in Flanders?' Lechasseur asked.

Edward nodded. 'Each of us is the second son in our families. The heir was too important to send on this quest, but us ... we have no place in society other than to serve our families. This adventure provides a purpose, a goal. Our brothers take care of our families, and when we return, we will have such glory that we shall be the ones who inherit all our ancestor's wealth, not our brothers.'

'Do you miss your families?' Lechasseur asked.

Edward nodded. 'We have been away far too long. It took

us six months to take Edessa. Six months, and that's hardly a strong fortress. There were more of us then as well, before Dorylaeum.'

'We lost many good men in that battle,' Peter explained, his voice low and croaky. 'And I fear we'll face similar hardship before Antioch falls.'

Lechasseur was impressed with the preacher's honesty. Most people he'd met here were defiantly ignoring the obvious, convinced that every trouble was a test sent from God and every success a reward, convinced that they would win out despite all evidence to the contrary. The crusader spirit was certainly indomitable, but just as much deluded. It was refreshing to hear home truths from the men on the ground.

'Relax,' he said, trying to reassure them. 'Once we get food and supplies from the city, your people will be refreshed. The people of Antioch can't hold out forever. They'll soon be just as hungry as you are. Besides, with me here to barter for you, you can't lose.'

Timothy thanked Lechasseur for his help, while Edward muttered something under his breath about being there to steal, not to barter.

As the party reached their entry point into the city, Lechasseur glanced around to see if anyone had seen them, but the night was quiet, and no Turkish guards seemed to be watching this section of the wall. Edward scuttled over to the base of the wall and pulled some branches and plant leaves away to reveal the secret gap that they were planning to use, a small alcove shrouded by shrubs and long forgotten to all but the crusaders who had stumbled upon it.

'How many people know about this entrance?' Lechasseur asked.

'Only a few,' replied Edward. 'We are careful not to use it too often, and every few days we send a spy to check if the Turks have discovered it.'

Lechasseur looked at the tiny hole, overgrown with plant life, and was not at all surprised that such a small breach had been overlooked by the city's inhabitants.

The four men squeezed through the gap and stood in silence to get their bearings. In the moonlight they could see rows of stone houses. Burning torches had been erected outside some of the houses, providing just enough illumination for the raiding party to see where they were going. In the distance was an imposing structure that Lechasseur assumed was a mosque, and the sound of a creaking mill could be heard from a different direction.

'We must keep quiet,' Timothy whispered as they began to trudge through the city streets. 'Although few will be awake at this hour, many will be stirred with the same hunger pains and nightmares we endure.'

Their journey through the city was uneventful. At one point they heard laughing and shouting coming from one house, but luckily no-one noticed as the crusaders crept by. They soon reached their target: a large, rectangular building where the last sacks of food were being stored and rationed.

'Spies tell us that the prince of the Turks has told them to be frugal with their food consumption,' Edward explained. 'They believe if they can survive longer than we can, we'll end our siege.' He sighed. 'They should not judge the people of God by their own weak standards.'

Lechasseur was beginning to find fairly tiresome the endless assumption that God was endorsing whatever course of action the crusaders felt like taking. He noticed that Peter the preacher, the one man he expected to be constantly harping on about God, was staying refreshingly quiet on the matter.

The party crept closer to the store but made sure to stay out of sight and earshot of the row of guards standing outside the building – no doubt on night-long watch to ensure none of the city's inhabitants took more than their fair share of the food. Lechasseur realised that getting in to the store was going to be difficult, and getting out with food supplies even harder. While he felt for the crusaders' plight, and was fairly ravenous himself, not having eaten since the day before, he didn't particularly want to steal food from the people of the city who, at the end of the day, had never asked to be besieged. Lechasseur had far more important concerns. He had arranged the raid in order to explore Antioch, and now he just wanted to find the old knight and figure out his connection to the forthcoming deaths. Then he and Emily could return home safely and eat all the food they could wish for.

'Come on,' said Edward, drawing his sword. 'This could get messy.'

'Wait,' Lechasseur said, laying his hand on Edward's. Killing in exchange for a few bags of grain might seem perfectly justified to the crusaders, but that didn't mean he was going to stand by while they did so. The way this raid was going, it was going to result either in their execution or in a quick success – neither of which would help him in his search for the knight. He had to come up with another plan.

'We're past the city gates now,' Lechasseur said. 'No-one's seen us, so we've time to develop a strategy.'

Timothy shook his head. 'I have my strategy, you fool,' he whispered. 'Kill the Saracens! Present company excepted.'

'We'll never make it past them,' Lechasseur said, ignoring Timothy. 'I suggest we find a place to hide, get some rest, then try again in the morning. If anyone asks, you're my assistants, my slaves if you like.'

Even in the darkness, Lechasseur could see that Edward's eyes were wide. 'You want us to pretend to be slaves to a Saracen? I would rather die.'

'In that case,' Lechasseur sighed, 'I fear you will get your wish. But if we succeed, then there's a good chance we can get as much food as we like – stealing their supplies not only from right under their noses but with their own consent!'

Timothy thought through Lechasseur's argument. After a couple of moments, he nodded. 'We will try your plan, but if it all goes wrong, *you* will be *our* slave forever!'

Timothy turned to Edward and the two smiled at each other, clearly thinking they'd reached a good compromise. Peter looked disturbed at the vassal's words. Lechasseur could do little but ignore their ramblings. They had a big day tomorrow and he now needed to find them somewhere to sleep.

As the sun began to rise over the city, the hustle and bustle of daily life began. While there was little food or water to be had, from the noise of the crowds it was clear that few in the city believed the siege would last much longer. Lechasseur was certainly struck by how much better these people seemed to be weathering the hardship than those camped outside.

They had spent the night sheltered under a sheepskin beside what appeared to have once been a market stall. Luckily no-one had noticed their emergence but a couple of nosy camels who took more than a little persuading to leave Edward's hair alone, much to the crusader's consternation.

Lechasseur had persuaded Edward, Timothy and Peter to hide their armour behind some bushes where it hopefully would not be found. They had rubbed sand into their hair, but when Lechasseur had pointed out that most slaves looked better-groomed than the vassals did at the best of times, they had decided to just get on with the plan.

While the city had only one set of main gates, there were numerous smaller towers that would most likely be less well defended. Lechasseur had overheard rumours among the crusaders that the commander of the one tower, the Tower of the Two Sisters, was not widely trusted and was believed to be sympathetic to the Christian cause. Perhaps this man could help them in their quest for a solution to the stalemate.

While they got a few odd looks as they walked through the streets, no-one challenged them, so it was not too difficult to reach the tower commander's office.

Getting an audience with the man, who went by the name of Firuz, proved harder, but the sight of the foreigners was unusual enough to pique the interest of his minions. They soon found themselves directed into his office. It was a pokey little hut, inside which a small man, wrapped in robes larger and more salubrious than anything anyone else was wearing, was seated at a desk poring over some documents. Firuz looked up as they came in. He had a bald head and little piggy eyes. In his late thirties, the man seemed slightly bemused by the early morning visitors, but was nevertheless intrigued to hear what they had to say.

'My liege,' Lechasseur began, doing his best not to sound intimidated by the situation, 'we are merchants from the Far East. We have noticed that all is not well in this city.'

Firuz gave a weary smile. 'It has been better,' he sighed. 'Ever since the invaders from the West besieged our city, we've had to suffer while we wait for assistance from neighbouring towns.'

Lechasseur nodded. 'We have seen your suffering, sir. We have also seen that the invaders suffer too.'

Firuz smiled. 'They will soon give up. Our willpower is too strong.'

'Forgive me if I speak bluntly,' Lechasseur said, 'but I fear stubbornness on both sides will kill you all. Please, send a contingent to negotiate a compromise. Surely you can work something out between the two of you, let the Franks who wish to settle here do so, convince their leaders that the problems they perceive to be besetting this town are just in their imagination?'

Firuz shook his head, his eyes showing he too had once thought as Lechasseur did. 'We have learned to our great cost that the Franks are animals; they don't think with logic as we do.'

'It is you who are animals!' barked Edward, outraged at Firuz's words.

'Quiet, slave!' Lechasseur snapped.

Edward looked furious, then paused as he remembered his role. 'I'm … I'm sorry. Master.' The words did not come easily to the poor vassal.

'Forgive my servant. He once served the Frankish princes who besiege you, but now he works for me alone. I've met many of them in my time, and while their exuberance and disregard for innocent life is well known, they do have a human side that can be tamed.' Lechasseur lowered his voice. 'If you send them some supplies as a gesture of goodwill, perhaps they'll be willing to talk.'

Firuz snorted, deriding Lechasseur. 'They are all butchers. They won't talk.'

'They're starving butchers. At least try to send an envoy. I realise you don't know me and can't trust me yet, but send someone you do trust. I'll guarantee their safety.'

Firuz leaned forward. 'How do I know you're not one of them in disguise?' He reached out, as if contemplating touching Lechasseur's skin. 'You certainly come from a distant land. You could have befriended the infidel on the way and decided to trick us.'

'To be honest,' Lechasseur responded, 'I couldn't care less if the Franks live or die. But they won't give up without a fight, and negotiating now, reaching a compromise before you all starve to death, will at least halt the suffering.'

Firuz gave a yawn and stretched his arms out before rising from his seat. 'Six bags of grain and vegetables, nothing more. You will tell the leaders of the Franks that if they want to take this city, then they'll have to pay a large price for me to hand over my tower. If all they want is to negotiate a peace, they should speak to our emir, Yaghi-Siyan. He will listen to their demands, but I doubt he will be able to agree to them.' He gave a Machiavellian smile. 'Oh, and please assure them that we're being perfectly respectful of their "relics".'

Lechasseur smiled and bowed his head in deference. 'Thank you, sir. I'm certain you'll soon be able to get your city back to normal.'

After leaving Firuz's office, Lechasseur sent Edward, Timothy and Peter off with Firuz's men to collect the food they had been promised, leaving him alone. He hoped he had done the right thing. His knowledge of medieval history was about as good as Emily's memory of her past, but by dealing directly with the parties involved, he had hopefully forestalled any possibility of his being executed by the crusaders as a Saracen. And now he had some time to do his own exploring.

He asked around in the market areas, but no-one seemed to

have seen anything of interest. Surely an elderly white man with a long, white beard would be a sufficiently unusual sight in the city to be remembered, wouldn't it? Still, he had got a couple of leads to areas where white men had allegedly been spotted. Their descriptions didn't really match that of the knight he had seen back in 1950, but every sighting of a white man was worth following up, he reasoned, even if it turned out that all that had been spotted had been the crusaders on one of their previous raids.

His first port of call was the home of a man named Kali who lived at the opposite end of the city, in the shadow of the imposing walls of the citadel. A fortress within the city, the citadel was supposed to be the last line of defence for the people of Antioch, an impenetrable refuge and hiding place to be used in times of strife. It was a testament to both the ineffectiveness of the crusaders' siege tactics and the resilience of the people of Antioch that more use had not been made of the place. But now, hundreds of people were gathered outside, desperately trying to get into the citadel to perceived safety. Guards were busy telling the crowds to go back to their own homes where they would be safer, but several skirmishes were breaking out amongst people who could not take no for an answer. Lechasseur wondered if these were scenes repeated daily, as the people became more and more desperate.

Lechasseur didn't want to get involved, so he asked someone on the outskirts of the crowd if they knew where Kali lived. One of Firuz's assistants had told him that Kali was an old white guy with a reputation for advanced scientific knowledge. It certainly sounded promising.

He followed the directions and soon found the dwelling. Smoke poured from the windows. Lechasseur feared the house was on fire, but after barging through the doorway and waiting for the cloud of smoke to clear from his vision, he found the old man fanning a pan over an old stove.

'Wretched thing caught fire again,' the old man grumbled. He reached for one of the stove's pans and tipped it over. A frazzled black lump of something that Lechasseur thought might have been chicken fell to the floor with a thud. 'Three days of supplies ruined!' the old man moaned.

He turned to see Lechasseur and looked surprised, then tried to regain his composure. 'What do you want?' he barked.

Lechasseur stepped further into the hut, and soon got a good look at Kali's face. He wasn't the man he was looking for.

'I'm sorry to bother you,' he said.

The old man hobbled over to Lechasseur. 'You're not one of us, are you?'

'You don't seem that bothered that your city is under siege.'

Kali shrugged. 'I've been here for most of my life, through Christian rule, Islamic rule, even a brief Pagan period … These things cycle round, and I just try to make the best of the situation.'

'I came here because I'm looking for someone. A knight with pale skin and a white beard, like yours. I thought you might be him, or at least might know of him.'

Kali wracked his brains. 'Sorry, I don't pay much attention to other people. They rather get in the way of my work, I find.'

'Could you tell me where the other white men here reside – the immigrant Europeans, like yourself? Is there anywhere where a white man who wanted to blend in could hide out?'

Kali looked at Lechasseur suspiciously. 'The Church of Saint Peter is a sacred place. If a Christian man was on the run, he would hide there.'

Kali's voice dropped, his tone becoming more serious. 'If you kill a man inside the church … it is considered an extreme violation. I should warn you that your man's compatriots would wreak a terrible vengeance.'

Reluctantly breaking off his search to rendezvous with the rest of his party, Lechasseur arrived back at the Tower of the Two Sisters to find Edward, Timothy and Peter just returning with a cartload of supplies. They were met by Firuz and his men. From beyond the city walls, the sound of distant trumpets could be heard.

'The Franks have left their camp to hunt,' Firuz said, cocking his ear to the sound. 'They are clearly desperate for food. But still

I have my doubts.' Firuz handed Lechasseur a sealed papyrus scroll. 'If there is a shred of decency in them, then at least they will read what I have to say and consider my words. If I am to break faith with my people, I will expect to be the richest person in the city once all this is over, with a life of unparalleled luxury. Assure your leaders, if they don't accept my offer, they will not live to see the next winter.' He looked up toward the city gates. 'Now go. Please.'

The guards began winching the tower gates open just enough to let the cart through. Lechasseur, intending to slip back later via the breach in the wall and continue his search, passed through first, thanking Firuz as he did so. Peter followed close behind. Edward and Timothy, however, were no longer with them. Lechasseur looked back over his shoulder and was aghast to see Timothy slicing into the guards with his sword. He looked up to see the tower burst into flames; a warning beacon to any who might see that the crusaders had arrived. Edward raced from within the tower, his arson complete, and drew his sword to join Timothy in battle. Firuz ran for safety, shrieking 'Infidel!' at the top of his voice.

Across the desert, from the direction of the crusader camp, a vast crowd was rapidly heading toward the city. Lechasseur could already hear the cries, the cheers, the gallop of horses' hooves … The crusading army was on the move.

The city gates creaked and moaned as they were winched open even wider. Lechasseur darted back inside the city, followed closely by Peter, and saw Edward straining to get the gates fully open. Two of the guards lay dead on the ground, while Timothy fought with another. Lechasseur was about to pull Edward away, but another guard got there first. Before Edward could move, a sword was thrust through his torso, sending him crashing dead to the ground.

With a riotous crash, the invading forces burst through the widening gap between the gates, the sheer force of numbers pushing them through. The wooden structures reinforcing the gates began to splinter and collapse.

Lechasseur grabbed Peter and pulled him to the edge of the

city wall to save them from being crushed by the incoming army. He paused to catch his breath, trying to take in what he was witnessing, then heard an angry, whimpering voice.

'You tricked me,' moaned Firuz. Lechasseur turned to see the little man cowering in a doorway. 'I was trying to help you!'

'No,' Lechasseur pleaded. 'I'm sorry. I didn't know ...'

Their conversation was cut off as the crusaders stormed the streets of the city, charging through any opposition and racing toward the temple where their spies had informed them the city's elders lay in wait.

'You must get to safety,' Lechasseur said, pushing Firuz away. 'If the city falls to the Franks, your life will be in danger.'

Firuz looked terrified. 'What can I do? How can we stop them?'

Lechasseur looked around, saw the wounded soldiers and heard the cries of the terrified townsfolk. 'Just be patient. Let them in, it's the only way to minimise the bloodshed. Get yourself to safety, head to the citadel, then summon help. I'll tell them you were killed in the stampede.'

Firuz reluctantly nodded, then slipped away down a side street.

Lechasseur's mind was in turmoil. How long had the crusaders been planning this? Weeks? Surprise was the key to any military victory, and Lechasseur's own ego had made him blind to the possibility that his expedition might be used simply as a convenient aid to the crusaders' own attack plans. He had been made an unwitting Trojan Horse, and he was furious.

'Are you coming with us, Saracen?' a voice said. It was Timothy, who was holding the reins of a horse, preparing to mount.

'Do you know what you've done?' Lechasseur demanded.

Timothy laughed. 'The Lord will repay us well. I'm going back to the camp to tell the others they are free to advance. Are you coming or not?'

Lechasseur shook his head. He still needed to complete his search. He swallowed his anger. 'Please, make sure Emily's safe and tell her to wait for me. I'll come back for her as soon as I can. I need to get to the Church of Saint Peter.'

Timothy nodded. 'I will tell Emily where you are,' he called, before galloping off towards the open city gates.

As Lechasseur made his way through the streets toward the church, Peter trailing along beside him, he could see the damage that the crusaders were causing in the city. Roofs had been broken and stripped, and many huts were burning in the morning sun. The bodies of those who had stood up to the crusaders lay on the streets. The people of Antioch had fought bravely, but they had been caught unawares. Facing an army on horseback, far more numerous than any they could muster, they had soon been defeated. Lechasseur wondered if Emily had been among the attackers, and briefly considered returning to the camp to check on her safety. But he knew the city would not be safe for much longer, and he had to try to find the old knight before he was cut off from this place for good. He had exaggerated his standing amongst the crusaders in order to curry favour with Firuz, but he knew full well that most of them wouldn't hesitate to behead him as just another ungodly Turk.

Back home, there were people who called Lechasseur a fixer. But a fixer made things better, made arrangements that improved people's lives. Sometimes a deal went well, sometimes not so well, but Lechasseur usually managed to work things out and make a profit in the end. Perhaps, he reflected, this had given him an inflated view of his own abilities. Some problems are too big to fix, even for you, he thought. He had tried to fix the situation in Antioch, believed he could mediate a truce, but instead he had become responsible for even more deaths, even more suffering. For someone whose view of time was not limited to the present, he had been remarkably blind to the possibilities of what the crusaders could achieve. He vowed not to be deceived again. He had to help put history back on track and make amends for his interference, then get back home with Emily and leave these people to their own destinies.

8

The fire crackled in the rapidly cooling mountainside air. Night was drawing in, and Emily didn't want to be around for too much longer in this climate. The tension was palpable in Godfrey's camp. Groups of soldiers of differing levels had been gathering, many polishing their armour and readying their horses. She had seen several arguments occur, one of which had ended up in a brief fist fight. Godfrey's army consisted of people from all over central Europe, and many clearly found it hard to leave their differences and prejudices behind them. The only thing that united the differing groups was the firm belief in the righteousness of their quest. Today the arguments had appeared more heated than usual. People were hungry and this was irritating them, but something else seemed to be on their minds, though no one would say what.

'It's getting cold,' Emily said to one of the other girls as they finished squeezing water out of an old tunic they had been trying to clean. 'Let's get this stuff inside.'

The other woman nodded and picked up the washing basket, moving it inside the tent. 'Why do you let them treat you like servants?' Emily asked. 'You're intelligent women here, but you let them walk all over you.'

The woman looked questioningly at Emily. 'Why are you always so quick to judge? Did it never occur to you that we choose to do these jobs?' She pointed to the gathering crowds. 'Look at them. The imbellis, the pedes, all ranks ... they fight on our behalf, for a noble cause. They need us in order to do that, and we're proud to be there for them. The men offered us the chance to leave many months ago, and many did, but those of us that stay realise the importance of the quest. We are God's army, and we play just as vital a role as those that lead the battles do.'

Emily regretted offending the woman, but was glad to see Simon at the back of the tent, having his armour adjusted. Much to her companion's horror, she walked straight over to him.

'Simon,' she said.

'Emily, can't you see I'm busy?' Simon scowled. 'What do you want?'

'What's going on, Simon?'

Simon took a deep breath. 'A fire has been seen burning in one of the city towers. It's a signal from our men … The gate has been opened, and we are free to take the city.'

'But Honoré …'

Simon sighed. 'Bohemond's army is already within the city, and we will be there too in a short while. I'm sorry, Emily. They are skilled soldiers. Your friend's chances of survival may not be high.'

Emily turned and walked quickly out of the tent. She had to get to the city, and fast.

She looked around and saw Timothy galloping up on horseback.

'Emily!' he called. 'I have news from your friend.'

'Timothy!' she said as he came up alongside her. 'I may need to borrow a horse!'

The streets of Antioch were ramshackle and arranged in a confusing manner, but Lechasseur eventually found the Church of Saint Peter, a curiously Christian outpost in a city in which, the Franks had assured him, the inhabitants had fanatically swept away anything connected with the faith.

The Church was a small stone building not too far from the citadel, with a long entranceway adorned by flickering candles and icons of the Disciples. As Lechasseur and Peter passed into the womblike depths of the building, the noise of battle and bloodshed outside faded, to be replaced with an air of contemplative silence.

The interior of the church was plain, with little decoration.

Several men wearing the hooded robes of monks were kneeling in prayer at an altar, which was laid out with a crucifix and burning candles, at the front of the nave.

One of the monks turned and stood as he heard Lechasseur enter. 'This place is for the followers of Jesus Christ,' the man asserted.

Lechasseur didn't have time for explanations. 'You know there are thousands of followers of Jesus Christ outside your city.'

The man shook his head in despair. 'They don't understand. We Christians may be few in number in this city, but we are at peace. We don't need their help.'

'You have been held prisoner,' Peter insisted. 'Of course you need their help!'

'I think it's a little too late to turn down the offer,' Lechasseur said. The other men praying turned round to look at Lechasseur. 'They've broken into the city, they're ransacking the place. You have to stop them. Someone has to stop them.'

One of the monks stood up and walked towards Lechasseur. His voice was rich and powerful. 'Today is not a time for sorrow, today is a great day!'

The voice seemed familiar, and Lechasseur turned his full attention to the man as he approached.

'Who are you?' Lechasseur asked. 'Do I know you?'

The man laughed. 'I don't believe we have met.' He began to lift his hood.

As the man's face was fully revealed, Lechasseur realised where he had encountered him before. It was the knight who had fallen from the sky in 1950.

9

Lechasseur had found the man he had been looking for, but something was seriously wrong. The man's beard was no longer grey and his face was far less lined. It was as if he was thirty years younger than when Lechasseur had last seen him, though with the piercing black eyes and distinctive facial bone structure, as well as the familiar voice, it was evidently the same man – either that, or a close relation. Lechasseur had worried that his time jump might have been a little off-target, but he had no idea he had got things this badly wrong.

'Who are you?' Lechasseur asked.

'I was once known as Reynald.'

'You!' Peter said, indignantly.

'You know each other?' Lechasseur asked.

'He is no monk,' Peter said scornfully. 'He is the Earl of Marseille, a traitor to the Christian cause.'

The man turned away. 'I have no family but the Lord.' He looked back and flashed a toothy grin at Lechasseur. 'And who might you be?'

'I'm a trader who got caught up in your little war unintentionally.'

There was a loud crash from outside, and Lechasseur and Peter were brushed aside as the men who had been praying with Reynald rushed off to see what was happening.

Lechasseur knew he had his man. Although he had not yet had a chance to explore Reynald's time snake, he detected the same feeling, the same air of arrogance. He was sure they'd jumped back to the time just before the knight or monk or whatever he was had travelled to the future, but as the man they'd seen in 1950 had been so much older, perhaps he had got the date wrong?

'You've had quite a journey, haven't you?' asked

JON DE BURGH MILLER

Lechasseur, wondering if he could catch a guilty look that might confirm his suspicions.

But the man returned Lechasseur's gaze levelly. 'I have travelled far to get here,' he said. 'And my journey is not yet ended.'

Lechasseur could see from the man's eyes that if he started asking about time travel, he would be wasting his time.

A familiar voice called from the church entrance. 'Saracen!' It was Timothy. 'We've come to get you. It isn't safe here any longer.' Timothy's words trailed off as he saw Reynald. 'You ...'

Before Lechasseur could stop him, Timothy had pulled his sword from its scabbard and was charging forward, clearly intent on running Reynald through.

At that moment, the church started shaking slightly, as if rocked by a minor earthquake, and a bright white light shone from nowhere to fill the room. When the light dimmed, Lechasseur saw to his astonishment that Reynald had moved safely out of the way of Timothy's charge, and in his place now stood a gaseous red apparition, a skeletal knight with its palms held out to Timothy, as if to welcome him to Hell.

Timothy slowed to a halt, his eyes fixed upon the monstrous sight. 'Lord save me,' he whimpered. 'What trickery is this?'

The apparition stood silently, the deep black recesses of its eyes staring invitingly at Timothy, beckoning him forward.

'The spirit of Saint Peter is calling to you,' taunted Reynald from the other side of the room. Timothy half-glanced to where Reynald stood, doing his best not to take his eyes off the ghostly figure.

From the corner of the room, Peter began to speak. 'You were exiled for practicing witchcraft. We should have killed you when we had the chance. What evils have you brought upon us, Marseille?'

Reynald smiled. 'Since I left those fools, I've learned many things. Many wonderful things, many terrible things. I've made discoveries to make you tremble, discoveries to make you weep.'

Reynald walked toward Timothy and from within his tunic took a long, tapering spike made from some pale material. He held the spike toward the apparition, and with a tormented scream, it shimmered and vanished.

The chapel was silent but for the sound of Timothy's heavy, terrified breathing.

'How did you do that?' Timothy whimpered. 'What power do you possess?'

'See this,' Reynald ordered, holding the spike out for Timothy to inspect. 'Take a good look.'

Timothy gazed at the object in Reynald's hand. 'There's blood on the end of it ... and an inscription ... a pentagram ...' He began to sob and backed fearfully away from Reynald.

'The Holy Lance!' Peter suddenly cried. 'The sacred relic used to pierce Christ's side during his crucifixion. You've found the Lance!'

Reynald chuckled. 'It found me.' His voice became a husky growl. 'The most powerful object in the whole of Christendom, and it found me. And to think you threw me out for being a heretic!'

'Oh God,' Timothy wept. 'Oh Almighty God.'

'Timothy,' Peter said. 'He is one of the devil's deceivers. We can't be sure he speaks the truth.'

Reynald ignored the preacher. 'My dear Timothy,' he said sternly. 'Do you remember the words of the Pope? What he told us that fateful day at Clermont?'

Timothy nodded and began to mutter through his tears. 'He said that the Turks had violently invaded the lands of the Christians, depopulating them by pillage and fire and looting them of all their treasures ... The Holy Lance of Christ, that which gives eternal life to all who are pierced by it, gone forever, robbed by the wicked race.'

'Eternal life,' said Reynald in acknowledgement. 'My gift to you.'

Timothy looked up, bewildered, as Reynald plunged the Lance into the side of his neck. A glowing field of energy surrounded the object and began to envelop Timothy. While Timothy's expression was one of pure shock, Reynald's face was a picture of ecstasy, and he held the Lance in place for several seconds before sharply withdrawing it. As he did so, Timothy collapsed to the floor, his face pulled into an expression of terror, and his body already starting to decay.

'Was that necessary?' Lechasseur asked grimly, taking a step toward the man.

'It's all part of my plan,' Reynald said. 'Would you like eternal life too, Saracen?'

'One life's enough for me, thanks.' Lechasseur backed away toward the exit archway. He had to find Emily and make sure she was safe. Was this guy really a native, or a time traveller fooling the locals with parlour tricks?

Reynald dismissed Lechasseur with a gesture and began to attend to the positioning of the cross and candles on the altar, as if nothing untoward had happened. 'It is said that Satan was cast out of paradise for tempting man, but it has recently come to my attention that God was unjust in his punishment.'

'So you're killing crusaders to make up for that oversight?' asked Lechasseur, pausing in the archway.

Reynald picked up the large, jewel-studded crucifix from the altar, admired it wistfully, then replaced it and walked towards Lechasseur, holding the Lance out in front of him. 'For centuries my family has guarded the Lance, and for many years now, a wonderful creature, more powerful than Lucifer himself, has spoken to me, guided me. When I told the Turks the location of the Frankish army at Dorylaeum, when I killed those souls most determined to recapture Jerusalem, I was doing his work. He speaks to me, and together we've found a way to return him to Heaven in the Devil's place, to become the true ruler of Creation. The successor to the fallen angel will become the risen master, with God as his servant.'

The Lance began to glow again, a green shadow surrounding it, while a grating humming noise seemed to emanate from its tip. Lechasseur looked closely at the object. It seemed to be made of finely carved bone and etched with symbols and pictures. It had been cut into the shape of a spear-head, and obviously matched the contemporary beliefs of what the Holy Lance looked like.

'According to rumour, you Saracens are in league with the Devil from birth,' Reynald said with glee. 'If that's the case, then I'm sure you'll soon be one of the chosen. With my help, you'll soon be part of our great army, ruling the heavens at my master's right hand!'

Reynald held out the Lance and lunged toward Lechasseur, trying to impale him through the chest, but the younger man managed to grab his arm and hold it back. As the two men struggled, Peter suddenly cried out. Distracted, Lechasseur momentarily lost his grip on his assailant, and Reynald pushed the point of the Lance home into his leg. A searing pain began to spread through Lechasseur, and drowsiness crept into his mind. He felt Reynald clasp a hand around his neck, and his vision filled with white as he saw the man's time snake. He had a confused impression of seeing a view from a rooftop, and experiencing a feeling of extreme sadness, before falling heavily to the ground. Then he was looking up at … looking up at himself. He was seeing himself, his own time snake, through Reynald's eyes. He could feel Reynald controlling the vision, taking him back through his life. He saw himself as a young man in the War, then as a child. Soon he was rushing back past his own birth, to the time of his grandparents and beyond. He saw generation after generation of his ancestors, rippling back through time, until the vision seemed to focus on one distant relative, a rejected and mixed-up child who grew up to be a man called Robert the Hunter, a man who would have two children. One of these children would eventually beget Lechasseur's forebears, while the other … the other was Reynald.

The vision dissipated and the drowsiness suddenly dispersed as Lechasseur felt the weight on top of him ease. He heard the thud of bodies falling to the ground and sat up to see a couple of large crusaders pinning Reynald to the ground. Lechasseur was breathing heavily as the implication of his vision began to sink in.

'Get up, then,' a familiar voice said.

Lechasseur stood up, turned around and smiled. 'Emily! I knew the cavalry would arrive sooner or later.'

Emily hurried over to Lechasseur and gave him the best hug she could, given the armour she was wearing. 'Sorry I'm late. My horse wasn't as fast as Timothy's. I take it your investigation has been a success, then?'

Lechasseur shrugged and looked down at Timothy's dead and decaying body. 'I'd say we had mixed results.'

Emily put her arm around Lechasseur's shoulder and helped him out of the church. His leg wound was painful, but he knew it wasn't too serious. He had to get it cleaned up soon, though, if he was to avoid infection.

'Hold him,' Lechasseur said to the crusaders, pointing at Reynald. 'He's the one who has been killing your men.'

The crusaders looked at Emily for confirmation. She nodded. 'Don't let him out of your sight. We'll be back before nightfall.'

'I will wait in the church,' Peter said. 'I need some time alone to gather my thoughts.'

'If things get dangerous, you may need to find shelter,' Lechasseur warned him.

Peter nodded. 'If I cannot make it back to the camp I will hide in the crypt, though it seems we have things in hand now.'

'Come on,' Emily said, helping Lechasseur away, 'let's find you some help for that leg, and you can tell me all that you've seen.'

10

Emily had expected to find the streets full of crowds of distressed civilians running in fear from the crusaders, and of Franks looting, pillaging and destroying the Muslim areas of the city. Instead, she and Honoré encountered body after body of crusader knights, lying slaughtered on the ground.

'The Turks must have fought back!' Emily muttered, shocked by what she was seeing.

They turned a corner and were confronted by a knight stumbling toward them, blood dripping from his mouth. Emily stopped the man, holding onto his arm. 'Where are you going?' she asked. 'What's happening?'

Emily could see in the man's eyes that he was frantic. 'It's … it's Kerbogha. The Saracen armies have sent reinforcements. We're no match for them. They're killing us!'

The knight pulled from Emily's grip and hurried away.

'We could go back home, you know,' Emily told Honoré. 'We could get your leg seen to by a 20th Century doctor.'

Lechasseur shook his head. 'No. Whatever Reynald's doing is clearly altering time. I've seen those people's time snakes terminate. Whatever chaos he's unleashing, we have to stop it now. We don't even know if there will be a future to go back to.'

Emily sighed. 'In that case, let's get you somewhere where we can bandage that leg.'

They made their way to the main thoroughfare through the city, but soon encountered pockets of battling soldiers from the two factions. Realising that they'd never get back to the camp safely while these skirmishes were going on – at least, not with Honoré's injury slowing them down – Emily decided to change tack. She led her friend to an alleyway behind a house. There she stripped off and discarded her crossed tunic, and placed her sword and Honoré's dagger alongside it on the ground. Then she concealed the whole bundle as best she could beneath a pile of earth. Putting her friend's arms around her shoulders and taking the weight off his leg, she led him back out of the alley and into the open, where there was still no sign of the fighting abating.

They hobbled over to a nearby house, and Emily pulled back the painted cloth that covered the doorway.

'Help us, please,' she said as she pulled Lechasseur into the building. 'We were caught in the fighting. They'll kill us if we don't find sanctuary.'

Inside, a large, middle-aged man was hurriedly trying to usher three young children into a back room.

'We won't hurt you,' Emily told the man. 'Please, we need help.'

The man stared at the travellers and saw Lechasseur's injury. 'Those animals did this to you?'

Lechasseur nodded. The man glared at Emily, then stood up and went into the back room, returning with several strips of cloth. 'Bind your wound then leave us in peace.' He looked at Emily. 'Your people are not welcome in this city. You have brought dark times upon us.'

Emily thought about explaining that she wasn't with the Franks, but time was short and the old man had clearly made his mind up long ago, so she settled for thanking him for his hospitality. He clearly thought they were mad, but in times of siege, neighbours frequently pulled together. It was the old Blitz spirit she'd heard of in London – you never knew when you'd be the next one needing the spare blanket from a stranger's house.

As Honoré sat on a stool and dressed his wound, he told Emily all about Reynald and what he had seen.

'And you believe all this Heaven and Hell stuff?'

Honoré shook his head. 'Of course not, but something strange is going on. Innocent people are dying, and I suspect we're the only ones who can stop him. He's a time sensitive, Emily. He saw my timeline, and I saw it through his eyes.

We're distantly related, it seems.'

Emily looked surprised. 'I take it the family reunion wasn't amicable?'

'We need to stop him, but we can't do it alone.'

Lechasseur tied the cloth wrap tight and flexed his leg experimentally.

'Will you be all right?' Emily wondered.

Lechasseur stood up and walked gingerly around the room. He gave a satisfied grunt. 'Emily, I think you should get back to the camp. Find Godfrey and the others, whoever stayed behind while this mess was going on. Get them to do anything they can to stop the madness. We need everyone to unite against Reynald. All the Muslims. All the Christians. Do what you can to get a force together. I'll come and get you when I'm ready.'

'Where are you going? You're in no fit state –'

'I'm fine,' Lechasseur said. 'If Reynald's a time traveller, connected or not to you or me, then I'm the only one who can understand him, the only one not blinded by all his religious mumbo-jumbo.' He laid a hand on Emily's shoulder. 'Please. Don't make a fuss.'

Emily glared at him, then pointed toward the doorway. 'Off you go then. If you don't come back in one piece, there'll be hell to pay!'

Lechasseur smiled, and limped out of the house. Emily followed him through the doorway, but turned in the opposite direction. She needed to find Simon.

Lechasseur returned to the church, expecting to find the place deserted. Instead, the green glow that Reynald's artefact had emanated now surrounded the small building. As he crossed the threshold, he felt a chill gust of wind, and the hairs on his neck began to prick to attention.

Inside the church, Reynald stood, arms outstretched, staring at the ceiling, his face bearing a fixed grin. Lechasseur looked up and noticed a circular hole in the roof. He hadn't noticed it before, but seeing how the light poured through it, he couldn't figure out why. There was no sign of the two acolytes, but Timothy's body still lay on the floor in the centre of the room, next to those of the guards who had been detailed to restrain Reynald. Of Peter there was no sign. Lechasseur hoped he had reached his hiding place safely.

'So you've returned!' Reynald whispered. 'I knew you would! You had a taste of the Devil's power, and now you want it for yourself!'

'Wrong again,' Lechasseur said. 'There is no Devil, there are no angels.'

'Look up there,' Reynald said. Lechasseur looked up through the hole in the roof, and saw that a storm was now brewing in the sky above. Rain began to patter down into the church, quickly forming sludgy puddles around the corpses. 'Do you know how long we've been without rain? The besiegers and the besieged. Heaven and Hell, locked in battle. But now … the knights have broken the city walls, the devils are slaughtering the knights. By bringing the Franks into the city, dealing with the tower commanders, you've brought balance to this conflict. Thanks to you, the energies I need to complete my work are flowing abundantly. My plan will complete ahead of schedule, and nothing you can do will change that. Perfection is close to being achieved. My destiny is set in stone.'

'Go on then!' Lechasseur said. 'Kill me, if that's what you want.'

Reynald turned to him, his eyes glowing like miniature balls of fire. 'It's too late for that. You had your chance.'

The rain began to cascade down even harder. Lechasseur felt it stinging his face, saw it making the marble floor of the church wet.

'Diabolus le volt!' Reynald shouted to the sky. 'Arise from the underworld, oh Lucifer.'

Lechasseur watched the spectacle with fascination. 'The only thing you'll summon is pneumonia.'

The rain was now torrential. Lechasseur was soaked

through. The noise of the water hitting the church roof was deafening. A wind was building within the church, moaning through its walls and foundations.

'You go by many names,' Reynald intoned through the storm, crying out to his God, 'but soon you will go by one name, as ruler of the Heavens.'

Lechasseur became aware of the buzzing of electrical pulses being carried on the wind. His vision was getting brighter, too, and bluer.

Reynald was shouting loudly as the rain bombarded him. 'The people will cry out in worship! Your name will become legend. My name will become legend!'

The blue light filled Lechasseur's vision and he felt himself slipping into unconsciousness. The last thing he remembered was Reynald turning to him, his voice scraping and maniacal, his eyes a fiery red, his face covered in blood. 'Everyone will bow before me,' Reynald croaked. 'Everyone will bow before my masters. Everyone will tremble when they hear the name Fendahl!'

11

Emily had expected to find the city gates defended by soldiers from one side or the other, but they were deserted and she was free to walk back from the city. It would be a long trek down to the camp unless she could find a horse, but she had to discover if Simon was still alive. He was the only one who could lend soldiers to fight Reynald.

As soon as she turned out of the city, Emily saw the body of a crusader. Young, no more than seventeen, he was clothed in the sketchy rags and filthy boots of an imbellis, one of Godfrey's cannon fodder. Ahead she could see more bodies, a number of riderless horses and several men on horseback patrolling the area.

As she neared, she could see that these weren't crusaders. She held up her hands to show she meant no harm. One of the riders noticed her and galloped over, speaking urgently in Arabic. The words were alien, but Emily understood what was being said. If she didn't want to be slaughtered, she would have to return to the city.

'I'm not a Frank,' she called. 'I come from the city to bring word to the Frankish prince Godfrey that his men have been slain on the altar of Saint Peter.'

The Arab soldier looked suspicious. 'Word has reached us by pigeon that Yaghi-Siyan is dead. It is the Franks who are the encroachers in our land, the Franks who chose to come here. If they suffer and die, it is no more than they deserve.'

'Please, let me through. I will beg the Franks to surrender to you.'

The soldier nodded. 'Kerbogha has told us to spare the women. Be on your way, but remember, before the day is out, the Franks will be known for nothing but the amount of their blood that has been spilled.'

Emily snagged the reins of one of the riderless horses and swung herself into the saddle. She galloped as fast as she could over the crusader bridge across the Orontes and soon reached Godfrey's camp. Clearly the forces of Kerbogha had attacked with ferocity, and a great battle had taken place. Emily surveyed the aftermath. The air was acrid, the ground treacherous, smoke and blood and ruin spread across the devastated camp.

The atmosphere was oppressive, a cloud of death hanging over the camp. Emily was disturbed to realise that she found it not so much uncomfortable as fascinating. The air of death was fresh, she could almost smell it. There was something so familiar about it; something under the surface that made her feel like she'd been in a situation like this before. She shuddered and hoped that all the things she'd seen whilst travelling with Honoré weren't immunising her to the emotional impact of such horrors.

Emily arrived at Simon's camp and dismounted. Simon was sitting outside the main tent with several of his advisors. Presumably they were discussing battle strategy. She went over to the group, and Simon smiled as he saw her approach.

'Simon, you have to help me,' she said, as soon as she was within earshot.

Simon looked bemused. 'What is it, Emily?'

'It's Honoré. He's found your murderer. He's a knight. Reynald of Marseille.'

Simon shook his head with resignation. 'Why am I not surprised?'

'He's trapped in the church inside the city. We've got him held down, but he's powerful. Honoré wants you, Godfrey, as many people as possible to come and help stop him. I'm not sure exactly what he's doing, but something big is happening, and I don't know how many of us it's going to take to end it.'

A rumble of thunder reverberated through the sky.

'Aimery!' Simon called to one of his vassals. 'Prepare my horse. I'm going to the city.'

The vassal hurried over and handed Simon a large cloak.

'Shouldn't you talk to Godfrey?' Emily asked.

'There's no time,' Simon said as the rain began to fall. 'Everyone's occupied fighting Kerbogha. I'll need to see this Reynald for myself before the strongest soldiers will come with me.'

Simon apologised to his colleagues and disbanded the meeting, before standing up and looking Emily in the eye. 'You shouldn't worry,' he assured her. 'I will deal with this knight and bring your friend home.'

They both looked up suddenly as a terrifying screech echoed all around them. There was a rippling in the air, and a monstrous creature resembling a giant snake appeared out of nowhere to tower above the tent. It had rippling rings of flesh encompassing its body, and a saliva-dripping jaw at its upper extremity containing several rows of piranha-like teeth ringed by a mass of writhing tentacles.

'What the hell is that?' Emily cried.

'The Devil's work!' said Simon grimly.

One of Simon's vassals drew his sword and lunged forward to fend off the creature. But the creature quickly reared its head and plunged it down on the back of the man's neck. He shrieked in pain as the life was literally drawn from him. Emily watched in horror as his skin wrinkled and clung to his bones in an instant. The snake creature released the man's body, which fell to the ground a mummified corpse. Another vassal approached, but ducked out of the way just in time, the creature's attack grazing across his body. The man fell stunned to the ground. The creature turned, shrieked again, then rose up into the air and plunged down head-first into the ground, boring through the soil and disappearing like a mole, though it was clear from the increasing transparency of its flesh that it was really disappearing more into thin air than into the ground.

The creature was gone. Emily and Simon looked at each other in astonishment.

'What was it?' Emily asked again.

Simon shook his head. 'It looked like one of the creatures of myth that captured Turks used to talk about. These myths strike fear into many of my men, but I don't know …'

The rain was now falling in torrents from the storm clouds above.

Simon ran over to where his injured vassal lay. He turned the man over and checked his eyes and his pulse. The man was somewhat wizened, as though even his minor contact with the creature had been sufficient for it to start to suck him dry, but he was still breathing.

'You will survive,' Simon whispered to the man. 'Please, stay with us.'

Emily saw the fearful expression on Simon's face and knelt down beside the injured man. 'We have to get him out of the rain.'

Simon nodded, and together they moved the man into Simon's tent and lay him down on a bed. The people in the tent had been huddled together, too afraid to investigate the noises from outside. They gasped as they saw what had happened to the vassal. 'Fetch him some water,' Simon called. 'And everyone stay inside. There are beasts of unspeakable danger on the prowl out there.'

Simon and Emily knelt down beside the vassal and did their best to comfort him.

Simon gripped the man's hand tightly, urging him to stay conscious. Emily was both touched and impressed by the devotion that he seemed to be showing to his follower. The crusaders faced death many times a day, yet Simon appeared far from resigned to it despite that. Emily found it hard to believe that he cared this much for every one of his friends who was injured, but looking at his eyes, she realised he did. The crusaders as a whole were a boorish people, but it seemed that inside every box of bad apples there was one good one; and, as she saw a tear run down Simon's cheek as he held his dying compatriot, she suspected she'd found it.

Simon turned to look at Emily. 'If those monsters are something to do with Reynald, then he might be more powerful than even you believed. I will warn your friend if I can find him. Please, stay here with Aimery, look after him.'

Emily moved close to Aimery, picked up a cup of water and put it to his lips.

'Bring Honoré back safely, will you?' she asked.

Simon nodded. 'I will be as quick as I can.' He looked over at Aimery. 'Goodbye, my friend.'

Simon left the tent and Emily turned back to her patient.

Several minutes later, another victim was brought in. Someone else attacked by a monster. Moments later, another. Then someone who had not been attacked by something unearthly, but who had been wounded in one of the battles with Kerbogha's forces. As more and more wounded soldiers found their way back to their camp, the pressure and tension in Simon's tent rose.

After almost an hour of doing all she could to make him comfortable, Emily saw Aimery shudder and pass away. She looked down at his body and wiped away a tear as she covered his face with a scrap of sheeting.

'I'm sorry, Simon,' she muttered under her breath. 'I did the best I could.'

She stood up and looked around the tent at the other soldiers being treated, some presumably also close to death. She had to do something to stop this. It was not in her nature to do nothing while other people took charge.

'I need to borrow some armour,' she called to one of Simon's other vassals. The man looked at her quizzically, but having seen the close regard Simon held for her and her angry temper, he clearly realised there was no use in arguing with her. He handed her a chain mail vest and she headed outside the tent, where the downpour of rain continued, and located the horse she had arrived on earlier. She was going to find Simon and Honoré, and together they were going to stop this madness.

12

Lechasseur woke to find a lizard perched on his face. He sat up quickly and the lizard tumbled to the ground before scurrying away. Lechasseur was immediately struck by the blood red sky, the constant splatter of rain on his face and the distant noise of what was either a thunderstorm or a battle being fought. For a moment he thought he was back in Normandy, but then he remembered Reynald's red eyes, burning into his soul.

Something swooped overhead, leaving a trail of fire in its wake. Had Lechasseur just seen an aircraft? No, not in the 11th Century. A meteorite, perhaps?

There was a hissing sound, and Lechasseur looked up to see a giant creature undulating through the sky above. It was part dragon, part snake, and left a sizzling band of flame behind it.

Lechasseur looked around. He was still in Antioch. He could see the Church of Saint Peter in the distance, but the streets around him were bathed in red light, giving them the appearance of being washed in blood. The heat was overwhelming. Lechasseur heard voices and turned to see a nearby arcade, which was covered with a tattered canvas roof. He struggled to his feet and darted under the canvas, to find a street scattered with broken carts and market stalls. He could see no-one there, and wondered whom he had heard. Was he going mad?

Returning to the rain-soaked main road, he saw a row of half-demolished stone houses, smoke pouring from several of them. As he passed by, the stench of rotting flesh assailed him. A deafening screech suddenly filled the air, and Lechasseur was almost knocked over as a large, horse-like creature with scaly brown skin galloped down the street, closely followed by a horde of rampaging knights. But these were knights like no others he had ever seen before. Their armour was constructed from bone and sinew, and Lechasseur saw that they had skulls for faces and a ghostly blue aura flickering around them.

He pushed himself as far as he could into the shelter of the wall of one of the houses as the fearsome group passed by, praying that they would not notice him. He hoped there was a sensible explanation for all this. He just had to keep searching until he found out what it was. He glanced down at his leg. It still gave him pain, but at least the bandage appeared to be holding.

Lechasseur's thoughts were interrupted by the scream of a young girl. He hurried toward the sound and found a child crouched sobbing beside the bodies of two civilians.

'Hey, easy there,' Lechasseur said, trying to comfort her. She turned to face him, then turned back to the bodies and continued to cry.

Lechasseur wondered what to do now, and looked up and down the road. A strange silence seemed to hang over everything, but then he heard the sound of something large being dragged slowly over the cobbled streets. There was a sucking, slurping sound too, something that raised the hairs on the back of his head. He had heard that noise before.

He grabbed the girl's arm and pulled her to her feet.

'We need to get out of here,' he said, and made to move off. His legs seemed rooted to the ground, however, and he remembered this feeling from before … this feeling of being trapped and helpless.

The girl suddenly screamed again, and Lechasseur looked up to see a massive, snake-like creature glide effortlessly around the corner in front of them. It was muscular and heavy, and exuded some form of slug-like ichor upon which it slid forward. Its head swayed hypnotically from side to side, and Lechasseur could see the ring of barbed teeth within its maw, surrounded by hundreds of seeking tentacles. The creature moved to the side of the street and smoothly up the wall of one of the houses there, sticking to the upright bricks and defying gravity. Its snout twisted toward Lechasseur and the girl, who were both struggling to break free of the paralysis that had overtaken them, and glided back down to the roadway, approaching them with an almost casual ease.

Lechasseur closed his eyes and concentrated on trying to make his legs move. He managed to get one, then the other, to stumble forward, and slowly, with the girl dragging behind him, he started to move haltingly down the road, away from the creature.

He heard the galloping of a horse, distant at first by drawing rapidly closer. There was a cry and the sound of hooves scrabbling on cobbles, and then suddenly Lechasseur found that he could move freely again. He looked around to see a horse and rider trying to spear the snake-like creature with a lance. The rider was struggling to control the horse, which was trying to bolt in terror. The rider managed to fling the lance at the snake, but even as it hit home, so the creature faded from sight, leaving nothing but a slug-trail of gently hardening slime to mark its passage.

The young girl pulled herself free of Lechasseur's grip and raced away down the road, vanishing into a side alley some way down. Lechasseur staggered over to the horse's rider, and recognised the man. 'Simon. Thanks!'

Simon nodded formally. 'Lechasseur. We were worried you might be dead. We haven't seen you since this morning.'

Lechasseur put his arms to the horse and began stroking its neck, trying to calm the skittish creature. 'What was that thing?'

'A Fendahleen. It feeds off fear. Only when it sensed that I wasn't afraid of it did it disappear.' Simon motioned for Lechasseur to get on the back of his horse. 'Come. We should find shelter from the monsters before they return.'

Darkness had fallen over the city, and Simon and Lechasseur had made a small fire inside an abandoned house. Keeping his voice low so as not to attract attention, Simon told Lechasseur of the terrible events that had occurred while he had been unconscious.

'We need to keep quiet. The forces of evil are everywhere,

listening. This morning, our knights took the city and all seemed well, but the Turks had a nasty surprise waiting. The armies of Kerbogha descended on the city, and the ensuing battle has claimed many lives on both sides. But we've all seen things – strange, ungodly things. There's more than just an Earthly battle being waged here.'

'I don't remember any of it,' Lechasseur said. 'I was in the church in the morning. There was a storm, in the church. I mean, inside the building.'

Simon looked into the middle distance, remembering. 'Yes, there was a storm. It was as if God himself was crying out for his people to stop their fighting, to stop the killing. You must have been thrown away from the church by the storm. It was more ferocious than any I've ever seen. But that storm was just the start of things.'

Lechasseur could hear the distant sound of people screaming, always on the threshold of his hearing. 'Go on.'

'Those monsters ...'

'What are they?'

Simon shook his head. 'The minions of Hell. That's what everyone says. But ... I don't know, I think there's something else. Emily told me what Reynald was doing –'

'Is she okay?'

'She's safe.'

Lechasseur stood up and walked over to a window. 'I remember something, the last thing Reynald said before I passed out. He was summoning his god, and he called it ... he called it Fendahl.'

Simon nodded. 'The Turks call the monsters the Fendahleen. It's what they cried when they first saw them. It's a word meaning minions of hell, servants of this Fendahl of which you speak. The creatures appeared in the midst of the storm, as if the rain was God's rage and this was Hell's answer to it.'

Lechasseur shook his head. 'Reynald must have summoned them, whatever they are. But where do they go when they disappear?'

Simon shook his head. 'No-one knows for sure. The Bishop

thinks that they're all connected, all linked to Reynald, the core of his Fendahl god. They're his eyes and his ears, and they seek out victims whose souls will be absorbed by Reynald's master. They've been killing without mercy. Christian, Jew, Muslim … they don't discriminate. There was death enough in this place as it was: we didn't need any more!'

'Why haven't more people left, if things are that bad?'

Simon shook his head. 'Many have, but many others see the tribulations we face as being proof of the Devil's desperation, tests from God himself. Stronger confirmation than ever that we are doing God's work, that this is God's will. "Deus le volt!" they cry. God wills it.'

Simon stood up. 'Reynald seems unstoppable; few are brave enough to confront him. Come. We must root him out of the church once and for all.'

'What makes you think we can stop him?' Lechasseur asked.

'There's more to you than meets the eye, Lechasseur. Anyone can see that. Search inside yourself. You have to be able to defeat him. You embody what little hope we have left.'

Lechasseur sighed. 'I wish I had your faith in me.'

Simon led Lechasseur out of the building and through the streets of the city, being careful to stay in the shadows.

'So, how many knights have you gathered?' Lechasseur asked.

Simon looked sheepish. 'Few will face Reynald. Most are busy outside the city fighting Kerbogha. Those that made it inside have been scared away by the creatures.'

Lechasseur shook his head. 'And you call yourselves soldiers. He's bound to have some weakness. We'll go to the church soon, but I need to find Emily first.'

Simon looked nervous. 'Honoré, I'm afraid I have not been completely honest with you. When I said that Emily was safe …'

Lechasseur looked levelly at Simon. 'If she's been harmed …'

Simon shook his head, his eyes showing longing. 'She is as safe as possible, but the Fendahleen are everywhere. Please, let me explain.'

13

Emily's horse slowed as she neared the city walls. Moonlight reflected off the long line of watchtowers surrounding the city, and she had to be careful not to be seen.

She dismounted and adjusted her chain mail tunic. The creatures inside Antioch had so far proved themselves to be ruthless, and if the crusaders were to consolidate their hold on the city in the face of the battle with Kerbogha, they couldn't afford to lose any more people, even apparent servant women like Emily. It seemed that word had got around about her prowess as a warrior. The crusaders now numbered barely a few thousand, the rest having died, deserted or settled along the way, but they were so close to their goal, there was a sense that it was only a matter of time before God finally rewarded them for their efforts.

This was not a place to stay forever. If the crusaders survived their current battles they would soon begin their journey to Jerusalem, something Emily definitely did not want to be around for. It was at times like this, separated from Honoré, in a completely foreign and confusing situation, that she really missed home. But a small voice inside her kept saying that London of the 1950s was just where Honoré lived, just where she'd settled after she appeared there one day as if from nowhere. It was no more her true home than this world of the 11th Century. But she tried not to listen to the voice. However she'd got to London before her amnesia set in, she had been put there for a reason, and whatever that reason was, she was sure Honoré Lechasseur had a part to play in her eventual destiny. As she stared up at the citadel of Antioch, and at the magnificent buildings that stood before it, she prayed that her friend was still alive.

Simon and Lechasseur arrived at the Church of Saint Peter and manhandled the heavy wooden door open.

'Reynald!' Simon called out. 'I know you're here somewhere!'

From the shadows at the edge of the room, Lechasseur heard a laugh and the clink of chain-mail.

A man stepped forward into the red light. It was Reynald.

'So you survived,' he said, impressed. 'After you disappeared in the time storm, I assumed the manifestations of my master would have killed you by now.'

'What are those creatures in the city?' Lechasseur asked.

Reynald smiled. 'For the return of the Fendahl to this world, several things are needed. Those creatures are part of that process. They feed off the energy created at the time of death, each one passing that energy to feed me in turn, giving me the strength to be reborn into my true destiny, the core body for the Fendahl. The creatures ensure we have a constant supply of energy until that time.'

'Your madness stops here, Reynald,' Simon muttered.

'And we haven't time to chat,' Lechasseur added.

From the corner of his eye, Lechasseur noticed a corpse lying on the ground. He recognised him from the crusader camp at Antioch. It was Eudes, another of Simon's vassals.

'I'm not the first one to try to stop you, am I?' he said.

Reynald smiled. 'Many believe that they can exorcise the devils within me, but they are all wrong, and they all die trying.'

'"Few will face him …"?' Lechasseur glowered at Simon. 'You lied to me, Simon. They have faced him, they've just all been killed!'

'I had to say something to make you come with me,' Simon insisted. 'If you'd known about the deaths, you would have kept away. But please, I know you'll succeed. He can't hurt you, Lechasseur.' He glanced at the corpse. 'You're not like the others.'

Lechasseur took a step back and began speaking quietly. 'No, Simon. There's more to it than that. How do you know so much? Why are you so desperate for everyone else to have a go at Reynald here. What's to stop you doing it yourself?'

'I …' Simon looked worried. 'I would, of course, but I'm just a humble servant of God. If I go near him, I'll surely die.'

'And I won't?'

'You're special, Lechasseur. You're different.'

'So you keep saying.' Lechasseur had long suspected that Simon had a hidden agenda, but now he was convinced. 'Every knight I've met here so far has been prepared to fight unflinchingly for his faith, convinced that he was assured of a better place in the afterlife if he happened to get killed.' Lechasseur looked into Simon's eyes. 'You're not a coward. I can see that. I have seen that. But there's something else going on. I think you're hiding something.'

Lechasseur reached out suddenly, grabbed Simon by the arms and spun him around. Caught by surprise, Simon toppled off balance, and Lechasseur pushed him stumbling straight into Reynald, like a bowling ball into a pin.

Reynald caught hold of Simon, and restrained him with one arm around his throat.

'Foolish knight!' Reynald said. 'Another victim for the Fendahl!'

'No!' Simon screamed. 'You can't do this to me!'

'You should have been warned away by the Fendahleen,' Reynald gloated. 'They're making sure that no-one interferes with my plan. As servants of the Fendahl, they're invincible. All their victims will soon become part of the most magnificent experience in all creation. But only the chosen few are transformed into Fendahleen themselves. Now you will have the honour of becoming the twelfth and final disciple. With you as a servant of the Fendahl, the gestalt will be complete and my master's summoning can be achieved!'

'What are you going to do?' Lechasseur demanded, but Reynald ignored him. The robed man raised his other hand, in which he held the shard of bone. He gazed at it in admiration, and slowly lowered it to press against Simon's neck.

'Hold still,' Reynald giggled. 'This may hurt.'

Lechasseur had suspected there was more to Simon than he was letting on, but had he been mistaken? Had he in fact just pushed the man to his death? He could only look on as Reynald dug the shard into Simon's neck, and Simon screamed in agony.

Simon's face seemed to be drawing in, getting thinner, as a green vapour appeared and surrounded him. Reynald smiled and held the shard in place.

Simon let out another cry, but then his voice quietened and he closed his eyes, as if he was preparing himself for death. The expression of pain seemed to lift from his face, and soon he seemed calm and composed.

Lechasseur stared at him, amazed. 'What's happening to you?' he asked. Rather than the life draining from him, as it had from those of the knights who had gone before him, his face seemed to be liquefying and breaking up, shifting like molten wax.

Simon looked up at Reynald, what was left of his face showing grim determination. He then reached an arm up and grabbed the older man around the neck. The bone shard clattered to the floor as Reynald tried to break free, but Simon began to squeeze, tightening his hold on the older man's throat. Reynald groaned, struggling for breath.

Lechasseur was impressed by Simon's newfound courage in the face of death. As he watched Simon's features continue to melt away and he saw the determination in his eyes, a realisation started to dawn on him. Unless he was mistaken, it seemed that the courage came from being the one in control of the situation. It wasn't Reynald who was causing Simon's skin to peel from his flesh, his flesh to peel from his bones, it was Simon who was doing it to himself.

Lechasseur watched, captivated, as Simon's now-exposed bones grew whiter, brighter, and began to burn like magnesium. Suddenly a magnificent aura surrounded him, a bright silhouette of white against the church wall. His back appeared to be growing, to be expanding, until, with a sound like tearing cloth, huge white-feathered wings burst free, pushing through his flesh and sending clumps of blood and muscle tissue splattering across the room.

Simon flexed the wings, stretching them out into the air like a hatching chicken, then used them to pull himself away from Reynald, who lay on the ground, shocked almost senseless by what he had witnessed.

Simon's form continued to change, his bones and flesh splintering, blood raining down as his old body was literally ripped apart, replaced with what looked like white robes, glowing hot and bright, illuminating the room.

The light spread across Simon's face, and gradually his human features began to reappear, making him look fresh and youthful.

It was the most powerful sight Lechasseur had ever seen, like a vision of Heaven, a creature combining an unspeakable beauty with a primal, alien form. It was intoxicating to look at, and impossible for Lechasseur to take his eyes from. He could feel raw emotion coming from Simon. A mixture of pain, joy, fear and hope. Lechasseur remembered the creature he had seen with Barnaby in 1921*. That had exuded the same sense of power and emotion and he felt honoured to be a witness to it. 'What are you?' he asked in awe.

Simon beat his wings, and they thumped powerfully in the air, lifting him several feet off the ground. 'I'm sorry you had to see me like this, Honoré Lechasseur.'

The creature that had once been Simon looked sad, dejected. 'You made a big mistake, Honoré. Like your friend, Emily, I have the gift of channelling time, of being able to move through it to do my master's bidding. I journeyed back from an era long after yours to help the people of this year, but my arrival caused a ripple in time that allowed the Fendahl to

---

* See *The Severed Man*

begin its manifestation. Now, I can do little except watch while the people I was sent to help bring about their own destruction.'

Simon swooped down until his face was inches from Lechasseur's. 'I know what you are, Honoré Lechasseur. I know you are no Eastern merchant. I know about you and Emily, travelling through time, changing history and interfering.'

'We don't interfere,' Lechasseur insisted. 'We just get caught up in other people's messes.'

'You interfered in my plans,' Simon sneered. 'I'm an envoy, sent back in time to ensure Reynald's defeat, to ensure this timeline did not occur. The Fendahl was not supposed to return for a millennium yet, but something happened. You changed history, Honoré. Reynald started his plan early, before I could find a way to stop him, and now the Fendahl has returned to bring death to the world!'

As Simon finished speaking, the ground began to tremble. 'The Fendahl approaches!' Reynald cried. 'Another victim must have been converted to a Fendahleen instead!'

The church began to shake as the earthquake grew stronger. Pieces of tile and mosaic began to flake and fall from the ceiling, unable to resist the stress. If the quake grew much stronger, the church would be in danger of collapsing. 'My plan is complete!' announced Reynald joyfully, rising to his feet. 'The Fendahl lives again!'

There was a bright flash of light and Simon surged upwards toward the roof of the church. Then he was gone, as if he had passed straight through it.

'Wait!' Lechasseur cried. His first instinct was to follow Simon, and it seemed that Reynald had the same idea. The hooded man snatched up the shard once more and darted through an archway on one side of the nave, disappearing up a flight of steps into darkness and presumably up to the roof. The church was shaking alarmingly now, and Lechasseur realised that moving to a higher level with the building on the point of collapse probably wasn't the wisest course of action.

But it seemed he had no choice if he was to stop Reynald and learn more about the creature Simon had become.

He raced after Reynald and eventually caught up with him as he reached the very top of the flight of stairs and stepped out onto a small ledge surrounding the roof, overlooking the city. Winds blew violently above the church, the force of the gathering storm increasing all the time. The Simon creature was hovering above, as if waiting for something. Lechasseur gripped the wall tightly as the earthquake continued to rumble.

'What the hell are you playing at, Reynald?' he cried. 'Get down from there.'

'My dear Honoré,' Reynald shouted over the rumbling noise, 'Hell is exactly what I'm playing at!'

Lechasseur was distracted as a familiar female voice called from the steps behind him.

'Honoré?'

From the shadows, Emily emerged, clad in a dirt-covered suit of armour, her hair knotted and grimy. 'I knew you were alive!' she said, rushing to give her friend a hug.

'I'm relieved you're safe,' said Lechasseur, returning her hug. He gestured to where Simon was hovering above them. 'You have to see this.'

Emily turned to the source of the screeching coming from her right and saw Reynald standing on the narrow ledge that encircled the domed rooftop, staring into the eyes of the creature that had once been Simon. Emily's eyes widened in awe. 'What ... what is it?'

'Simon. He ... he had more than a couple of secrets.'

Emily studied the being before her. Like an angel, or a tornado, or a monster ... She looked at the expression on the creature's face and somehow knew that Lechasseur wasn't lying. This was indeed Simon.

'How ...?'

'Whatever he is, I think he's a time channeller.'

The blood drained from Emily's face as Lechasseur's words sunk in.

'Look at my work,' Reynald shouted back at Lechasseur and Emily, pointing across the city. The view was terrifying. Burning buildings, mounds of corpses strewn around like beacons, all under an angry crimson sky. 'All this glory, all to prepare for the coming of the Fendahl, and now that moment has arrived!'

Reynald lifted up the shard he'd been using to extract the life-force from the soldiers. 'Show yourself in me, oh ancient one, I call you forward to fulfil your destiny.' He held the piece of bone high above his head and began chanting in a tongue that sounded to Emily like something less than human.

The storm raging far above in the clouds seemed to descend, the noise increasing to a deafening level. As Reynald continued to chant, a bolt of lightning shot forth from above and struck the roof near him, but no damage appeared to have been done.

Reynald turned to face them, his eyes now orbs of pure black, his hair writhing like snakes, his body glowing, illuminated in a bath of bright gold light. 'The moment of summoning is complete!' he announced. 'The Fendahl lives once more!'

'Not if I can help it,' Emily cried, pulling her sword from its scabbard and lunging forward towards Reynald. Reynald's reactions were quick, and he too drew his sword. He swung the heavy weapon round to parry Emily's blow, and it seemed that she had lost her advantage.

'Foolish girl,' Reynald shouted. 'You can't stop the Fendahl!'

The blood-red sun was setting, the skies darkening, the storm clouds above swirling frantically.

'Well it can't hurt to try!' Emily said, flinging herself forward and into Reynald, doing her best to push him over the edge of the parapet. Reynald grasped hold of Emily and attempted to steady himself, his feet scuffing at dust on the ledge, knocking pebbles of rock down to the ground far below. Then he fell backwards, and Emily went over after him.

'Emily, no!' Lechasseur cried as he saw them begin to fall,

helpless to do anything to stop it. He reached out, hoping to be able to touch Emily, so that they could jump through time to safety, but she was too far away.

But then time seemed to freeze, like a photograph. Looking on in astonishment, Lechasseur realised that Emily and Reynald were still falling, but only by a miniscule amount each second. Was this his time sensitivity going into overdrive, he wondered? Was he himself frozen in time, immobile as he had been when the Fendahleen approached? But then, as the storm fired another bolt of lightning down to the roof, he realised it wasn't frozen time he was witnessing. Emily and Reynald were clashing on a psionic level, locking each other where they were, both time travellers, both equally powerful. Sparks of blue electricity began to circle around the warring duo and a gust of wind, a miniature cyclone, surrounded them.

'Help her!' Lechasseur cried to the angel above, watching in horror as Emily hung in mid-air, just moments away from meeting a bloody end hundreds of metres below.

'I can't touch him,' the creature that had been Simon insisted. 'She must do this herself.'

Emily screamed.

'Fight him, Emily,' Simon urged, flapping his wings and circling the warring duo. 'You can do it if you believe you can.'

Emily's mind was in turmoil. On the edge of her perception she could see the ground far below, the battered city of Antioch. In the centre of her vision was the craggy face of Reynald, staring wildly into her soul. His eyes had merged with the time storm, the phenomenon she had encountered before only when jumping through time with Lechasseur. As their minds touched, she felt a moment of true kinship, and saw Reynald's naked soul in a way few others ever could. It was at that moment that Emily realised what Reynald was. He wasn't a time channeller like her, he was a time sensitive, like Lechasseur. He was trying to push her away, force her to the ground below, but she fought back, using her mind as well as her physical energy. She didn't understand quite how it was that they had come to be suspended in mid air, but she somehow knew it was as much her doing as Reynald's. But he was strong, and she could not fight him for much longer.

'I can't do it!' she cried. 'I can't stop him!'

'Feel the power of the Fendahl,' Reynald hissed. 'Listen to what you feel inside. You know it to be true. Feel the sweet taste of death, the beauty of destruction.'

Emily felt a torrent of memories pouring into her head. She saw death and destruction choreographed into a beautiful opera, whole towns laid waste in a perfect creation of chaos. She felt hungry, ravenous for human souls, for the joy that death would bring her. She saw reality through the Fendahl's eyes, felt what it was like to feed off death, and she liked it.

She smiled at Reynald. 'Yes, the Fendahl ... Show me more. Let me taste it!'

'Save her!' Lechasseur cried again at Simon. 'You must be able to do something! She shouldn't have to die for your cowardice!'

'Emily, please. He's trying to trick you.' Emily heard Simon's voice in her mind, telepathically willing her on. She had to resist Reynald's games – all he was doing was planting thoughts in her head, trying to fool her into accepting that the Fendahl was the rightful owner of this planet.

'It's okay, Simon,' she cried, as she felt the destructive energy of the Fendahl wash over her, 'I can see my destiny now!'

'No Emily, he's using you!'

Emily saw a vision of the battlefield, of the hundreds of crusader knights and their families lying dead. No, this was all wrong. She found the sight intoxicating, addictive, but she wasn't going to let Honoré end up like that. In her heart, she knew it wasn't time to aid the Fendahl quite yet.

'Get out of my mind!' she screamed. She turned to look back to Honoré, and called out to him. 'He's a time sensitive. I'm going to jump.'

The warring couple fell several feet closer to the ground, their power over each other weakening. Reynald reached for Emily's throat and began to squeeze, choking the life out of her.

'She can't!' Simon cried. 'They'll spread the Fendahl's influence across time!'

'Goodbye Honoré,' Emily shouted, tears in her eyes.

'No!' Lechasseur yelled at her, but he was powerless to stop her.

The angel, however, wasn't.

'What have I become?' he heard the angel mutter under its breath. The creature had a terrified yet determined expression on its glowing features. It turned and steeled itself before moving directly toward Emily. The bright light surrounding Simon enveloped Emily and Reynald, who both screamed in agony as it did so, their heads jerking skyward, mouths open as they gasped for breath. Simon seemed to fly straight through them, merging his own body with theirs. 'It's the only way!' Simon cried, though the voice seemed to come from everywhere at once.

The maelstrom of energy continued to surround Reynald, suffocating him and keeping him and Emily in the air.

A long white tendril extended from within Simon's back and wrapped itself around Emily. Holding her secure, it then spiralled out toward the ledge where Lechasseur stood, placing the girl out of harm's way beside him.

Lechasseur and Emily hugged once she knew her footing was sure, and turned to watch the spectacle unfolding before them.

'Come with me!' Simon cried as Reynald struggled to break free. 'Come with me through time!'

Blue electricity sparked around Simon, and the tornado surrounding them appeared to dissipate.

'They're going to time jump!' Emily muttered.

'I don't think so,' Lechasseur said. 'Look at Reynald.'

The knight's face was contorting in agony, but he was resisting Simon's urges. 'I'm going nowhere,' he growled.

'Forward through time!' Simon cried. 'Forward!'

Reynald's face was changing, lines deepening on it. His hair was greying, whitening. 'I'm not going with you, I belong here!'

Simon's anger was palpable. 'You have never belonged here!'

Emily realised what Simon was doing – by trying to force Reynald with him into the future, he was provoking Reynald to resist, and that was causing the knight's body to age, taken forward in its personal timeline while physically staying in the 11th Century. The process was accelerating now, and Reynald's body would surely die soon from the shock of the experience.

'I thought you said you couldn't kill him?' Lechasseur shouted over to Simon.

'I can't!' the angel cried. 'But I can suppress the Fendahl influence within him, at least for a while.' Simon's energy continued to merge with Reynald's, but as the knight grew older, the angel grew smaller, until there was little of him left. It was as if their bodies were becoming one.

Then there was a loud bang and a burst of light, and the gestalt Reynald-Simon entity careered toward the church rooftop, crashing onto the walkway next to Lechasseur and Emily. From the sky where the two had been fighting, the remains of Simon's human body, reduced now to chunks of flesh and bone, fell to the ground below. The light dimmed, and almost at once the storm started to abate.

Reynald crouched on the walkway, a withered husk of his former self, struggling to breathe, shivering violently. Lechasseur moved over to him with trepidation. He cautiously reached down toward the man. Reynald looked up at Lechasseur, a bewildered expression on his face. The only trace left of Simon was the burning light in Reynald's eyes.

'Easy,' Lechasseur said, trying to reassure him. 'Everything will be okay now.'

Reynald bared his teeth and stood up. 'What have you done?' he growled. 'The Fendahl was supposed to rule the Earth!'

He threw a punch in Lechasseur's direction, but Lechasseur blocked it, the impact knocking Reynald, who had underestimated his weakened physical state, off balance. As the two men connected, Lechasseur glimpsed Reynald's time snake once more. He felt cold, like someone was walking over his grave, and realised that his time snake was likewise being read by Reynald. 'Help me,' Reynald cried, his eyes whitening. Then he lost his balance and toppled backward, away from the ledge. He started to fall, but as he did so, blue electricity crackled all around him, and in a flash of power, he disappeared completely.

14

Once Reynald had disappeared, the ground stopped shaking immediately. Lechasseur and Emily peered over the edge of the church rooftop, looking for any sign of the prematurely aged knight, but there was none.

'Is he dead?' Emily asked, after a while.

Lechasseur shook his head. 'It's Simon. He's taken Reynald to the future to save his life. Separated from the Fendahleen, the Fendahl will hopefully be powerless, will return to whatever part of Hell that it and its creatures came from.

'So at least we know now how Reynald came to appear in 1950. I think Simon's set the whole thing up so that I'll meet Reynald on that street in London and we'll be drawn back here to the 11th Century. He's created a loop in time, so that we're sort of destined to go through what just happened.'

'But is already *has* happened, hasn't it?' said Emily, struggling to grasp her friend's theory.

Honoré shrugged. 'What came first, the chicken or the egg?'

They stood in silence for several minutes, staring out over the city, reflecting on what they had endured.

A ghostly Fendahleen flew by trailing fire and screeching in defiance, but powerless now to cause any more death. Without Reynald, without a core element to control them, the creatures were nothing more than phantasms born from crusader nightmares. The Fendahleen spun towards Lechasseur and Emily, as if seeing them as its next meal, but before it could near the church, it broke up into small black particles of ash that fluttered away on the wind.

Lechasseur bent and picked up the shard of bone that had been left resting on the ledge. It was cool and seemed innocuous now. He followed Emily back down the stairs.

'Lechasseur! Lechasseur!' a voice called as Lechasseur and Emily emerged into the nave. It was Peter, the preacher who had accompanied Lechasseur on his raid into the city and hidden in the recesses of the church as Reynald's plan had been enacted.

'Peter. What is it?'

The preacher ran up to Lechasseur. 'Is it over? Have we won?'

'Not quite,' Lechasseur looked at Peter and handed him the shard. 'Marseille left this, and you may be able to use it to inspire your people on to victory.'

Peter smiled and clutched the fragment to his chest. 'I must tell the others of this find. Whether it is the Lance of Christ or not, it is clearly an object of power. With this on our side, Kerbogha's men will surely soon be defeated!'

Peter raced from the church as fast as he could, a broad grin on his face. Lechasseur and Emily smiled at each other. 'Do you think it's safe to give him that?' Emily asked. 'The Fendahl influence ... it's irresistible. It's scary. For a moment there, I think you lost me.'

Lechasseur was less concerned. 'I knew you'd come through. Reynald took the Fendahl with him, wherever he went. The Lance is harmless now that he's gone, nothing but an old piece of bone.'

As Lechasseur and Emily ventured out into the city, normality, or at least what passed for it, seemed to be returning to the place. With the monsters gone, the crusaders had left to assist their armies fighting Kerbogha outside the city walls, and the extra manpower, combined with the inspiration from Peter's so-called Lance, would soon turn the tide of battle in their favour.

The aftermath of the city's troubles – the attack from the crusaders and the battles with the Fendahleen – made Lechasseur and Emily nauseous. All around the streets were corpses, pools of blood and dead animals, but few of the knights left in the city seemed to be bothered by what had gone on. They all seemed more concerned with getting back to the battlefront and securing the victory that God had promised them.

Emily and Lechasseur found Simon's steed outside the church and made their way through the city on horseback, returning through the gates to Godfrey's camp. The camp was far enough away from the fighting to be safe. They pulled up outside Godfrey's tent and dismounted. As they did so, a booming voice called out to them.

'Saracen!' Lechasseur turned. It was Godfrey. 'I thought you were dead along with the rest of your kind.'

'It's over, Godfrey,' Lechasseur said.

Godfrey nodded. 'Yes, or it soon will be. We took the city, now we'll defend it. I have renewed faith that the Lord is on our side. Did you see how we slaughtered the devils? How the angels themselves and all the menagerie of Heaven came down to aid us, just as we knew they always would?'

'Many people died, Godfrey. How can you celebrate that?'

Godfrey shrugged. 'The heathen were punished, the holy were martyred. It has been a glorious few days.'

Lechasseur's face was grim. 'Godfrey, we found your murderer. He won't be troubling you any longer.'

Godfrey smiled. 'Yes, I can feel it in the air. As if an evil presence has been lifted from our midst. You are free to go, Saracen.'

Lechasseur put a hand on Emily's shoulder. 'Come on.'

After recovering their clothes from the ditch where they had hidden them, they headed off to find a way home.

'Did we do the right thing?' Emily asked as they walked. 'Has history been altered?'

Lechasseur shrugged. 'Perhaps we were always meant to intervene.'

'But you told me what Simon said. The Fendahl wasn't supposed to reappear for another millennium.'

'If he's right, the Fendahl was supposed to awaken a few years after our time. If I'm right, then we've stopped that happening.' Lechasseur looked out over the battered crusader camp. 'The damage here has been terrible, but can you imagine what would happen if the Fendahl was brought back in the 20th Century, in a city like London, a place with atomic weapons?'

Emily shuddered.

Lechasseur's face looked cold. 'Come on,' he said, 'we've still got to find a way of getting back home.'

Emily smiled. 'I think I know a good place to start.'

Emily led Lechasseur to a nearby tent where one of Godfrey's servant girls was holding a baby, one of the children born on the crusade.

'Hello Edith,' Emily said. 'Hello baby William.'

The woman looked up at Emily in surprise. 'Emily? We thought you had been killed.' The girl noticed Lechasseur and was clearly disturbed by his presence.

'I'm fine, Edith. This is Honoré. He's a friend.'

'Hello Edith,' Lechasseur said with a smile. He looked down at the infant. 'Hello William.' He reached out a finger, which the baby clasped, while with his other hand, he reached out to grasp Emily's. He saw the baby's time snake clearly, and smiled, pleased to see that it extended for many decades. The Fendahl's influence had been stopped. He looked at Emily and smiled again. They held hands, and blue electric sparks began to bounce around their bodies as the winds of time propelled them forward into the future.

Reality coalesced, and the greeney-yellow smog of London was revealed. After several jumps through the centuries, finding baby time-snakes to read in order to travel the maximum possible distance each time, Lechasseur and Emily had finally arrived back in London, 1950. It was early morning. Although the street lights still shone, so did daylight. They had overshot their exact point of departure by some time, and when they located the spot where they had left the fallen Reynald, there was no sign of the knight. All they found was Lechasseur's discarded backpack, which he picked up and threw over his shoulder. 'We have to find Reynald,' Insisted Lechasseur. 'Just in case he kills anyone else ...'

Emily placed a comforting hand on his arm. 'You weren't to blame, you know. Anyone would have made the same decisions.'

Lechasseur ran his hand through his tightly-curled hair. 'All those deaths ... I've been a fixer for years now, but what for? What really matters is, I couldn't fix it for those people to live.'

'History is cruel,' Emily said. 'And time is crueller.'

'We flit around, getting by, doing deals and living a good life, but to what end? We travel through time, see things most people could never imagine, yet sometimes I just feel like we're going round in circles.'

He looked at Emily. 'Sometimes I think I'm cursed. For years I've felt different, seen time in a different way from others. It's something that's been in my family for centuries. But now I've seen what I came from ...'

'You don't know –'

'I do. I think I knew the moment I first touched Reynald's mind. I'm the same, and I don't want to end up like that. When our minds touched, when he read my time snake, then for a brief moment our memories merged. I saw his future, I saw him looking up at me after he fell from the roof. And I saw my future, what will happen soon, but ...'

'What is it? What did you see.'

Lechasseur sighed. 'I saw nothing, Emily. Nothing at all.'

'Like there's nothing in my past?'

'That's different.'

Emily shook her head. 'No it isn't. You're a good man, Honoré. We choose our own destiny, we choose what we become. It doesn't matter where we came from. It's what we do now that matters.'

Over the next couple of days, Lechasseur and Emily purchased every newspaper they could find and took them back to Lechasseur's flat, where they scoured them for references to the knight. Lechasseur had called in favours at the local hospitals, but no patients fitting the older Reynald's description had been admitted. On the third day, Emily found one snippet in the *Mail*, an article on the troubles workers for the new National Health Service were facing, and how many of them were complaining that their pay wasn't as good as it had been when the hospitals ran as private operations. To illustrate the problem, the article mentioned one ambulance crew who had admitted a frail old man in the middle of the night after an anonymous tip off. Upon opening the ambulance doors once they reached the hospital, they had found the man gone. Emily wondered if, despite his injuries, Reynald had been the absconding patient, and had managed to jump through time yet again.

'But where would he go?' Lechasseur asked, when Emily mentioned her theory.

'Simon was strong,' she suggested. 'Whatever he was, whoever sent him, he didn't belong in 1098. Once the Fendahl had been defeated, he would have been called somewhere else. Perhaps back to his people.'

'To the future?' Lechasseur took a sip from a cup of tea, pondering this. 'Perhaps Simon is strong enough to drive the Fendahl out completely.'

Emily shook her head. 'I hope so. But ... I felt it, Honoré. It's powerful. Reynald wouldn't give up without a fight. I don't know whether Simon or Reynald has the upper hand, but if the Fendahl survived ... I think solving the crusaders' problem might have done little but send the Fendahl somewhere else in time, create a new problem for someone else to deal with.'

'But like you said,' mused Lechasseur, 'Simon's strong. He wouldn't give up without a fight. As long as he lives, the Fendahl can never return. I think the only thing we can do is just try to forget about it now. We'll learn the truth one day, I'm sure.'

Emily hoped her friend was right. She worried that even he didn't really believe what he was saying. Still, there was no use worrying about something that might never happen.

'You were right about Simon,' Lechasseur conceded. 'He was a good man. Or whatever he was.'

'But so afraid of his true nature. In the end, though, he couldn't deny his history.'

There was an uncomfortable pause.

'Do you think I was working for a power from the future too?' Emily asked. 'Before I came here, I mean. Do you think Simon held the key to my identity?'

Lechasseur shrugged. 'I doubt it. You're more human than he ever was.'

Emily sighed. Honoré, she reflected, just didn't understand her. Her curiosity about her past had burned unbearably for months. But now, after what she had seen, she was starting to wonder if some things were boxes best left unopened. She'd seen extreme sadness in Simon's eyes, and hoped she would never have to suffer such feelings herself. She'd tasted death and destruction through the Fendahl, and discovered that they somehow fascinated her; a deeply unnerving realisation. She hoped such thoughts would never surface again. Either way, there was little she could do about it. Tomorrow they'd put their experiences in 1098 behind them and start afresh. Perhaps that was for the best. Perhaps that's what all this was about. Time heals, so they say, and time travellers have more healing to do than most.

That evening, Emily said goodnight to Honoré and made her way home through the darkening streets, thinking again about Simon's fate and wondering if she would ever have to face the secrets of her own past …

Acknowledgements

Thanks to the Gesta Francorum, Anna Comnena, Fulcher of Chartres and the University College London library. Additional thanks to Mark Clapham, Ed Greenall, Jim Smith, the writers of the other *Time Hunter* books and extra special thanks to my family, especially my parents, John and Mary, for endless love, support and encouragement.

About The Author

Jon de Burgh Miller lives in London where, in addition to writing, he runs an internet consultancy company and is a keen student of medieval history.

Jon's previous work includes the novel *Doctor Who: Dying in the Sun* for BBC Books, co-authoring *Twilight of the Gods* for Virgin Publishing's New Adventures series, as well as several short stories in collections such as *Missing Pieces* and *Short Trips: Repercussions*. Over the years Jon has written for several cult TV magazines including *The Official Xena: Warrior Princess Magazine*, *Doctor Who Magazine* and *Cult Times*, as well as numerous fanzine articles.

The Time Hunter Series

Book 0 – *Cabinet of Light* by Daniel O'Mahony

Book 1 – *The Winning Side* by Lance Parkin

Book 2 – *Tunnel at the End of the Light* by Stefan Petrucha

Book 3 – *The Clockwork Woman* by Claire Bott

Book 4 – *Kitsune* by John Paul Catton

Book 5 – *The Severed Man* by George Mann

Book 6 – *Echoes* by Iain McLaughlin and Claire Bartlett

Book 7 – *Peculiar Lives* by Philip Purser-Hallard

Book 8 – *Deus Le Volt* by Jon de Burgh Miller

Book 9 – *The Albino's Dancer* by Dale Smith

Book 10 – *The Sideways Door* by R J Carter and Troy Riser

Book 11 – *Child of Time* by George Mann and David J Howe

Printed in Great Britain
by Amazon

65127933R00068